MW01227631

Behind Skye's Eyes

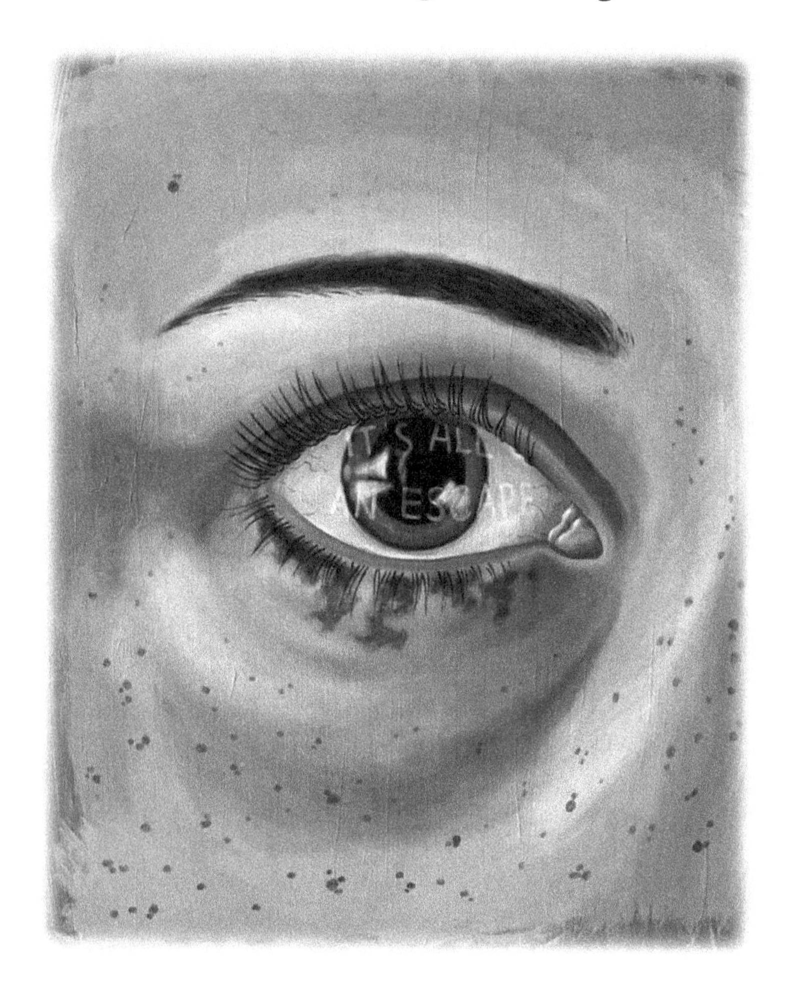

By

Rebekah BT

ISBN:
Hardcover: 978-1-962381-14-7
Paperback: 978-1-962381-13-0

DEDICATION

I dedicate this book to those battling addiction, homelessness, mental health, loss, and trauma. To the ones who have lost a loved one to addiction. To all the frontline workers who are fighting this crisis every day and doing the best that they can to help the community. To all the volunteers and donors, you make an incredible difference in the community. To the ones that I have lost to addiction: Alexandre, Antonio Jr., Derek, Christopher, Jessy, Ben, Adrian, Darling, and more and to the ones still here, lost and trying to get back on track: You will get there. I see you. I hear you. I acknowledge you. I respect you. I love you. You are worthy. You are enough.

ACKNOWLEDGEMENT

I would like to acknowledge and thank everyone who has been by my side, supporting me through this journey of writing and healing. I love you all.

To my mom, Sylvie, and my dad, Dave, thank you for encouraging me to follow my many dreams and goals, no matter how crazy they are.

To my family and friends for always believing in me and for loving me and my weird ways. Thank you for your support, love, and kind words, and for still being there even though I am the worst at keeping in touch.

To my coworkers and friends that I made in this community, you guys are all legends and heroes. I know times have been hard, and some of you have been around for way longer than I have; kudos to you. Shout out to everyone on the front line and to the community for not giving up and fighting back. I want to take this opportunity to acknowledge everyone who has been affected by the depths of this issue, mentally, physically, and emotionally. We are here to do the best that we can, but we cannot save the world. Remember to take care of yourselves first and foremost in order to support yourself and the community in the best ways that you can. You are also important, and your health matters. Remember to step away when you need to recharge. We are all in this together.

I would like to thank my amazing and talented aunt, Heidi Taillefer, for collaborating with me and creating the cover for my book. If you haven't Googled her yet, do it now. (Thank me later.)

I would like to thank my dear and talented friend, Danielle Gillard, for collaborating and walking with me while taking beautiful shots of the DTES. (DownTown EastSide)

I would like to thank my amazing friend Brittany Vaughan for letting me use her study paper on opiates and Fentanyl. Thank you for all that you do for the community and the animals.

I would like to thank my talented friend from high school, Justine Bélanger, for collaborating with me and painting her view on the things spoken about in this book and for seeing the beauty in darkness and melancholy.

I would like to thank Artie, my cat and my little guy for being with me while I hibernated in my apartment writing this book. You kept me sane (for most days). Thank you for your collaboration by stepping on my keyboard a million times.

CONTENTS

ABOUT THE AUTHOR

Rebekah, a passionate writer and advocate, was born and raised in the vibrant city of Montreal, Quebec. However, her journey eventually led her to settle in the beautiful coastal city of Vancouver, British Columbia. Rebekah's life took a significant turn after she completed her studies in sound engineering and graduated in 2015.

Having always had a deep love for music, Rebekah initially pursued a career in the music industry. She worked on various projects and immersed herself in the creative process, but her path would soon take an unexpected turn. The devastating loss of many friends to drug addiction shook her to the core and ignited a profound desire within her to make a difference.

Motivated by her personal experiences and fueled by her compassion for those struggling with addiction, Rebekah decided to shift gears and dedicate her life to helping people in need. In 2021, she embarked on a new journey as an Outreach Worker in the Downtown Eastside, a neighbourhood in Vancouver known for its challenges with poverty, homelessness, and drug addiction.

Rebekah's work on the front lines of the addiction crisis exposed her to the harsh realities and heartbreaking stories of individuals battling with substance abuse. Despite her best efforts to provide support and assistance, she encountered traumatic events that had a profound impact on her own well-being. It was during this challenging period that Rebekah recognized the healing power of writing.

Finding solace and catharsis in the written word, Rebekah took a hiatus from her outreach work to focus on her personal healing and embarked on a new path as an author. Drawing from her experiences and the stories she had witnessed, she began writing a novel that blended fiction with elements of truth. Recognizing the potential impact of her words, Rebekah poured her heart and soul into the project, dedicating herself to raising awareness and breaking the stigma surrounding drug addiction.

After just four months of intense dedication and tireless writing sessions, Rebekah completed her first novel. The characters' names were changed to protect their identities, but the story itself was rooted in the authentic events and emotions she had encountered throughout her journey. At the age of 33, Rebekah found herself at the beginning of an unplanned writing career, driven by her desire to shed light on the reality of addiction and inspire open conversations about it.

Through her debut novel, Rebekah aimed to challenge preconceived notions, educate society, and foster empathy for those affected by addiction. She wanted to give a voice to the often-marginalized individuals she had encountered, shining a light on their struggles, triumphs, and the complex web of factors that contribute to the cycle of addiction.

Rebekah's ultimate goal was to dismantle the stigma surrounding drug addiction, encouraging society to approach the issue with compassion and understanding. She believed that by humanizing the stories of those affected by addiction, she could inspire change, promote healing, and foster a greater sense of community.

As she embarked on her writing career, Rebekah embraced her newfound purpose with unwavering determination. She understood that her words had the power to touch hearts, challenge perceptions, and spark conversations that could lead to meaningful change. Through her novel, she aimed to leave a lasting impact on society, contributing to a world where addiction is understood as a human struggle rather than a moral failing.

Rebekah's journey from a music enthusiast to an Outreach Worker and now an author exemplifies her unwavering dedication to making a positive difference. With her powerful storytelling and commitment to destigmatizing addiction, she strives to ignite compassion and empathy within the hearts of her readers, ultimately forging a path toward a more inclusive and supportive society.

ABOUT HEIDI TAILLEFER: BOOK COVER ARTIST

Heidi Taillefer, a talented artist born in 1970, has called Montreal, Quebec, her home throughout her life. With a diverse artistic career spanning over three decades, Heidi has made significant contributions to both the commercial illustration and fine art realms. By 2004, Heidi had made the decision to dedicate her full time and energy to her fine art projects.

Heidi's works have received acclaim internationally, with her exhibitions attracting art enthusiasts and collectors from around the world. Her pieces have graced the walls of esteemed galleries and museums, showcasing her ability to provoke contemplation and engage viewers on a profound level.

Through her art, she invites audiences to embark on a journey of introspection and exploration, blurring the boundaries between reality and the ethereal. Within Heidi's artistic journey, a special connection exists with Rebekah, her niece. Their bond extends beyond family ties, as they share a common love for artistic expression and a mutual understanding of the transformative power of art.

You can follow her on her Instagram account: @heiditaillefer Website: https://www.heiditaillefer.com/

ABOUT DANIELLE GILLARD – PHOTOGRAPHER

Danielle Gillard, a talented and passionate photographer, hails from the enchanting city of Yellowknife, Northwest Territories. With a deep appreciation for both portrait and landscape photography, Danielle captures the beauty of the world through her lens.

Currently residing in Vancouver, British Columbia, she is actively pursuing her career as a photographer and embarking on new artistic ventures. As a portrait photographer, Danielle has a remarkable ability to capture the essence and personality of her subjects. Her images convey a sense of intimacy and connection, drawing viewers into the emotions and stories encapsulated within each frame. Danielle's friendship with Rebekah serves as a source of inspiration, encouragement, and collaboration in their artistic pursuit.

You can follow her on her Instagram account:
@daniellegillardphotography
Website:
https://www.daniellegillardphotography.com/

ABOUT JUSTINE BÉLANGER - ARTIST / PAINTING

Justine Bélanger, born and raised in Montreal, Québec, possesses a deep passion for acrylic painting and has developed a distinctive style that is both vibrant and melancholic. Her art serves as a reflection of her emotions, experiences, and the world around her. While settling into her new city, Justine's path converged with that of Rebekah, a familiar face from their shared high school years. The reunion sparked a rekindling of their friendship, allowing them to reconnect and support each other in their respective creative endeavours.

You can follow her on her Instagram account: @jujubelange

ABOUT BRITTANY VAUGHN - WRITER FOR FENTANYL & OPIOIDS STUDY

Brittany Vaughn is an ambitious student at Simon Fraser University (SFU), where she is currently pursuing her master's degree in Psychology. With a deep passion for understanding the human mind, she also works as an outreach worker in the Downtown Eastside. It was in this role that she had thepleasure of crossing paths with Rebekah and starting a supportive friendship.

WARNING!

This book contains sensitive and potentially distressing content, including discussions of drug addiction, suicidal thoughts, and sexual abuse. These themes are explored within the narrative and could be emotionally challenging for readers who have personal experiences or vulnerabilities related to these topics. Reader discretion is advised, and it is recommended that you engage with this material in a safe and supportive environment. If you find yourself becoming overwhelmed, please consider reaching out to a mental health professional or a trusted individual for support. Your well-being is important.

If you or someone you know is grappling with addiction, suicidal thoughts or homelessness, please remember that you are not alone on this journey. Reach out for help; people and resources are available to support you. Remember seeking help is a sign of strength, and there's no shame in asking for support. You have the power to change your circumstances, and there are compassionate individuals ready to guide you through this challenging time.

Picture Credit: Justine Bélanger

Page Left Blank Intentionally

CHAPTER 1

FILLING THE VOID

I can hear his drunken laughter coming from the living room, alongside the cigarette smoke dancing its way through the cracks of my bedroom door. Ever since Mom passed, he has spent all his time drinking cheap whiskey and watching TV in his cigarette burnt recliner. We don't talk like we used to. Sometimes, it feels like he can't even look at me because I am a mere reflection of her. He wasn't always like this. Only sometimes when he drank too much at family dinners or on other random nights. Now, it's every day. I miss him. I miss how things used to be. The day my mom died, I lost both my parents.

They were high school sweethearts. Mom was extremely timid and kept mostly to herself. She was on the swim team and dedicated most of her time to this passion. As for my dad, he was the typical high school jock, always causing mischief while using his charm to get away with it. Mom claims she was utterly disinterested in him. Meanwhile, he did everything he could to impress her and catch her eye. Dad swears he knew she was the love of his life from the moment he saw how annoyed she was with him.

He had always loved a good challenge. I remember waking up in the morning as a kid on weekends to the sound of jazz music playing in the kitchen, accompanied by the smell of fresh coffee. I would silently creep my way through the hall and hide behind the wall facing the kitchen table. I would wait for him to notice, and he would follow with, "*Is that a little mouse I hear?*"

That was my cue. I would then run into the kitchen, sit on his lap, and watch him do his crossword puzzles in the morning paper. The easy ones would rub him the wrong way. He would always say, "*Come on! What is this? Crossword puzzles for morons?*"

Mom would laugh, shake her head, and kiss his forehead, reminding him that he says this every weekend yet continues to do it. Now, some mornings when I wake up, I close my eyes and go back to these moments.

Life was good back then. Everything made sense, and I felt like a normal kid. Mom made Dad the happiest; even though he was becoming a grumpy old man, she would keep him grounded. I feel bad for him. Part of me also resents him for giving up on me. I was 15 years old when she crossed over to the other side. I felt so lost. I watched her suffer so much that I remember almost wishing she would go sooner rather than later. But when she did, I felt guilty, angry, and betrayed. Mom and I were close. We told each other everything. Sometimes she would feel bad because she felt like she shared too much with me for my age. It's probably true, but I feel like that's also what made us so close. She was my best friend. I did feel my dad's jealousy emerge when my mom would take my side, but he shrugged it off as he knew better than to go against us.

When Mom crossed over, that's when everything turned to shit. My dad and I barely spoke anymore, if not at all. I was on my own from then on. I would go out with friends and come back at all hours of the night. I would stumble in, wasted and high on the MaryJane, and most times, he wouldn't even notice me. Other times I would sit at the park down the street from my house and watch the sunrise on the upper limb, just above the horizon, caressing my cheeks with its warmth. This calmness reminded me of life when Mom was still here. She always spoke about her infatuation with the mysteries of what was beyond the sky; her favourite saying was, "*The sky is not the limit; there is so much more if you just let yourself be free and fly.*" She says that is why she named me Skye because I could be everything and more with no limit. We don't speak much about her. When I try, he barely responds, as if she is a distant memory from another life. I still write to her, not every day, but when I miss her or when I want to share moments or accomplishments. It makes me feel closer to her. At times, I even write what I believe she would respond to. She always had the right words to calm the storm in my mind. Why did God rob her from me? Is there even really a God? I am doubtful of this because, if there was, would there be so much pain and misery inflicted on humanity? If there is a heaven, as they claim, then we must be living in hell on earth.

After Mom's death, I was able to do whatever I wanted; Dad never questioned my whereabouts. At the time, I thought it was great; I had the most freedom in my circle of friends, but eventually, it started to weigh on me. I craved a better balance. I wanted my father to care about me while still giving me the freedom I had. But instead, I got freedom and nothing else. I say freedom because, at the time, that's how I saw it, and that's what I would tell myself to feel better. I realize now that I was in denial of the neglect and feelings of abandonment that I was suppressing. It took me a couple of years to fully feel the effects of it and realize the truth that I was blindly walking through.

For example, when he missed my graduation, I had to come up with an excuse as to why no one from my family was there to celebrate with me. I could distinguish the looks of pity and judgment from the other parents. *Poor young renegade running amuck drinking and smoking weed while her father drinks all day* is probably what they were thinking. They aren't wrong about that, either. I was in a phase of experimenting with booze and weed with the older kids as I was making my way through high school. I am here, though, standing among my classmates, graduating, and finally getting away from this stupid high school filled with douchebags and douchettes.

The summer of graduation was when Alex and I started sleeping together. It was nothing serious at first; it was a friend I was comfortable experimenting sexually with. Alex was not like the other stupid boys in my school. He was emotionally aware and very knowledgeable. He would spend hours passionately talking to me about things he had read on the internet.

Meanwhile, I would try to keep up, nodding my head with a faint smile to appear as if I was following. I call it "The Mona Lisa" smile. It works like a charm. I would get lost just watching him be so passionate about the most random things. I was secretly envious of him. I wished I could be like him, as I don't feel much excitement for things besides him, booze and weed. He had noticed my general lack of enthusiasm and claimed I should go talk to a professional about depression. I personally find it useless, knowing the doctor will solely prescribe me anti-depressants, and then I will be more numb than I already am. *I self-medicate with marijuana and alcohol,* and that's what I tell him every time he brings it up.

I had gotten a part-time job as a waitress at a diner. It wasn't very busy or known, but it was the only place that would hire a 17-year-old with no prior waitressing or work experience. I figured working here could open doors for better restaurants after a year or so. The restaurant was owned by a Greek family. They were sweet but also very cheap. I would notice pay cuts here and there, but I never said anything because they always fed me for free.

It was nice being around a family since I did not really have one anymore. The love and drama they had amongst each other were quite entertaining, and they treated me like family. I lost my job eventually, though, when I began to do no-shows. Alcohol and weed became my main priorities once I began to dabble in drinking and smoking. They let me go with no hard feelings, understanding that I was at an age where I would begin to discover certain hobbies and boys.

I remember the first time I smoked a joint. It was with my high school friend Stew. He was two grades above me. I was in eighth grade at the time. We decided to skip class to hang out by the football field and *smoke some reefer*, as he would always say. I remember feeling a little nervous but mostly curious. I had heard many kids in my school talk about getting high but had yet to experience it myself. He had rolled it up before we got to the field, and he claimed that this was not his best roll. The joint looked like it could use a little TLC, but what did I know? I was the noob here.

He lit it up, took a big hit, and instantly coughed all the smoke out. His coughing fit lasted for almost a minute, which then made me doubt the whole thing. He explained that the more you cough, the higher you get. *Fuck it, why not?* I thought to myself. I took the joint, held it like I had seen in the movies with the index and the thumb, and brought the joint close to my lips. The smoke went up in my nostrils, which then caused my eyes to burn and water. Stew laughed at me while still trying to catch his breath. As I took my first hit, I held it in for about five seconds and then released the smoke. I only coughed a little—nothing like Stew, though.

That day, MaryJane took me to ***La La Land.*** Everything appeared so different and weird. I felt some anxiety arise, but then I would forget about it and find myself distracted by whatever was around me. The giggles were my favourite part, along with the munchies afterward. When I got home, I went straight for the fridge. I opened the door and stood there for about 15 minutes, gazing at the little food we had. Luckily, Dad hid his chips in the freezer, so I took the bag into my bedroom and ate the whole thing. He wasn't too happy about it, but he got over it quickly after the fourth beer hit him.

Later that year, Stew convinced me to look through my dad's liquor cabinet and bring a bottle with me to school for us to drink. Looking at his collection, I was trying to find one that would be easy to replace with water. I read one that indicated *Gordon's London Dry Gin.* The liquid was clear, so it was going to be easy to add water to the bottle, and my old man wouldn't notice anything missing. I ran to the kitchen to look for a marker to mark a checkpoint for the refill. I poured some Gin into an empty water bottle with the help of a funnel, then filled the Gin bottle back up to the mark and placed the bottle back in the cabinet.

I arrived at school, and I spotted Stew sitting by the steps, probably waiting for me in hopes that our plan had succeeded. Once he saw me, he smiled, and I gave him a thumbs-up. He gave two back, grinning from ear to ear.

"*Hey! Did you manage to get something?*" he asked excitedly.

"*Hey, Stew! Yes, I got some Gin London, something Dry,*" I boasted.

"*Nice! I've never tried that before; I wonder what it tastes like. Did you try it?*" he wondered.

"*No, I didn't, but I did smell it. It smells strong and piney. Like the cleaning product my mom used to use when she would wash the floors. Also, it was easier to replace the missing alcohol with water,*" I explained.

"*That's fair; hopefully, we aren't drinking floor cleaner then,*" He teased as we made our way into the school.

"*Meet me at lunch break by the football field. I'll bring the snacks since you brought the drink,*" Stew offered.

"*Cool, see you then. Good luck on your French quiz, ya dweeb,*" I cheered.

That day I learned four things:

I hated the taste of gin.

Alcohol can make you black out.

Don't drink at school.

You might do things you regret while drunk.

I don't remember the first time I had sex. I'm glad it was with Stew, though, and I wish I could remember it. It's like it never happened—for me, anyway. Stew remembers it all, or so he says. I've asked him to tell me the details to see if it would bring any flashbacks, but nada. He claimed it was great but a little sloppy and awkward, which would make sense considering our state.

Stew and I stopped talking after he graduated. I still wonder what he is up to, hoping one day he will reappear in my boring old life.

CHAPTER 2
DULL FACE

It's Saturday evening, and I'm lying on my bed, scrolling on my cellphone until it starts vibrating. Emily is calling, most likely to make plans for us to get befuddled with the booze and the herbs. Any reason for me to get out of this depressing hole is good enough. I picked it up.

"*Hey Em, what's up?"* I started.

"*Skye! What are you up to? Feel like hitting up a rave tonight?*" replied Emily excitedly.

"*Woah, kind of last minute, but sure, why not. Who's playing?*" I answered eagerly.

"*Tonight's headliner is Alix Perez! Hence, I called. I know how much you love his music,"* she said, her enthusiasm was clear in her voice.

"*What! No way! Fuck yeah, I'm totally in. Have you called Lilly yet?*" I returned the answer with the same zest and inquired about Lilly.

"*No, you know how she is with last-minute plans. Especially since we want to go to a rave, she might be weird about it,*" she replied dejectedly.

"*Let's do a 3-way call and try to convince her to stop being such a suss,*" I reasoned.

Emily adds Lilly to the call.

"*Lilly Shmilly! Get your granny pants off, and let's go get silly!*" Emily yells.

"*What! Where? I just put my pyjamas on,*" Lilly replies, unmotivated.

"*Come on, Lils, Alix Perez is the headliner! We can't miss out on this!*" I reply.

"*Alix, who? I have no idea who he or she even is. I've had a long day and was just about to watch a movie in bed.*" Lilly still sounds dull.

"*Oh my god, what are you, 80 years old? It's Friday; put something sexy on, and let's get lit!*" Emily answers, somewhat annoyed.

"*Fine, fine, simmer down, will you? Give me an hour, and I'll meet you both at Emily's.*" Lilly finally agreed to accompany us.

"*Amazing. See you both in an hour*," said Emily with a cherished tone.

Click. Emily hangs up.

"*Skye?*" Lilly remains on the line.

"*Yeah, Lils, what's up?*" I answer.

"*Can we please not stay out until the sun comes up? I'm mostly going to keep an eye on you girls. I know how Emily can influence you at times,*" Lilly replied back with concern.

"*Oh, don't worry about me! I know she can be intense, but it's always a good time in the end, no?*" I assured.

"*I guess. I'm not in the mood for her to be on my case all night; I'm just letting you know,*" she snarled.

"*Yes, yes, I know, Lils, I got you. Now get out of your pyjamas, G-mama, and let's have a good night, okay?*" I laughed.

"*Yeah yeah... I'll see you soon,*" She sighed.

Click. We hang up.

I stepped in front of my mirror and apathetically observed the details of my physical appearance. My long, dark curls, dehydrated from the monthly pharmacy hair dye sessions, are way overdue for a trim.

"*Maybe I should just cut it all off,*" I said out loud while trying to find a way to make my hair look decent enough. I sighed, staring at my empty green eyes, supported by my tired eyelids and dark circles. *A little bit of concealer will do the trick.* I thought. Growing up, I often felt insecure about many things, especially my freckles. Now, they make me miss Alex. We agreed to return to our friendship status after almost two years of dating. It was hard for me to feel like myself again after Mom left us. Alex was always there for me and ignored my passive-aggressive comments. He is always able to see beneath the surface.

I always loved that about him. But I can say I took that for granted toward the end of our relationship. I became complaisant with his will to always put me first. Eventually, it got old, and he was slowly taking his distance. I knew what he was doing, but my ego let my stubbornness take over. I kept convincing myself that he would always be there until he wasn't. It's been a year now, and we have found each other again. But not as lovers, as friends. Some days I miss the old us, but I know he deserves better, and I will only taint him with my haunting, ominous thoughts. He loved my freckles. He would always ask to draw star constellations with them, and I always refused. I don't know why I never let him; I regret it now. Sometimes I draw constellations with my fingertips, and I picture his touch instead of mine. It takes me back to the safe place I once had with him.

I always lose focus when he infiltrates my thoughts. Okay, back to analyzing myself. My lips looked torn and dry from biting them so much. It's a weird habit I have; I'll bite off the skin until my lips bleed. I guess it's my anxiety speaking. It's weirdly comforting to replace one pain with another. My old man tells me it makes me look like a junkie when I do that. I hate when he uses the word "junkie." Who is he to judge with his beer breath and sloppy words?

I looked out my window and noticed the sunset looking beautiful yet angry this evening. A light red with tints of orange slipped through, filling the gaps. "I feel you," I whispered. The colours reminded me of the pain and anger I've been swimming in. It felt like that sunset was a rumination in my soul. As I stared at the sky, I felt myself slipping into the vortex of my thoughts.

And I know it's not what's best, but I am thankful for anyone who would bend over backward to extend a hand to lend. I am thankful for my friends to fall back on when the world lets me down. I am not delirious; I'm serious when I say I won't stray from a path that is taking me somewhere, a destination unknown.

There is no time to be uptight, a warrior who wonders where the wisdom lies when silent cries fall on deaf ears. These eyelids led to the tainting of a young mind. There is no such thing as time, as everything is purely an illusion that serves as some type of comfort to our kind.

The thoughts in our minds turn into coloured clouds, reflecting our pure vibrations. Sensations that reside yet cannot be explained by words, but only by these tints of colours we paint. Quantum physics at its finest.

I hear Dad slam the beer fridge, which brings me back to reality. I opt to begin scanning my options in the closet, bored with every piece of clothing I own. I need to go shopping; I can't remember when the last time was. I am pretty sure that my attire is outdated. I know it is. I just couldn't care less. "*When in doubt, wear black.*" Easy peasy. I picked out my favourite black leather skirt and a ripped-up T-shirt I've probably worn over a hundred times this year. The countless holes each have their own story, so why not keep adding? I throw on some ripped-up black stockings, apply some light makeup, put in my 15 earrings from my countless piercings, switch out my nose ring to my favourite snake-looking one Alex bought for me years ago, slip on the leather skirt along with my shirt, and *voilà*! Now I just needed some mascara, and I was good to go.

Next step: I still need to acquire my party favours. My go-to recipe for these nights is usually ye old gin, Maryjane, accompanied by a little bit of snow white. I am my father's daughter. Therefore, my alcohol tolerance is quite impressive until it kicks me in the face with a blackout. This is when Mrs. White comes to great use; she keeps me tamed. As for mary-jane, well, she simply keeps me sane.

Jax always had the good stuff, or so he claims. He's the only one I know who has what I need, and most people I know call him when they need some supplies. He's also easy on the eyes—that is until he opens his mouth. It's a shame when that happens. The universe creates this lavish human yet forgets to dazzle it with some intelligence. I guess we can't have it all. Even beautiful, smart people deal with some type of bullshit. Or I would like to think so. How would I know? I was blessed with none of the above besides bullshit, bullshit, and more bullshit.

The phone vibrated. It was Emily.

"*What time is it? 9:12 pm. Shit. I'm late,*" I said to myself.

I answered the phone.

"*Sorry, Em! I didn't see the time go!*" I responded regretfully.

"*You need to work on a new line! Just hurry up! We're waiting on your slow ass. I'm getting antsy!*" Emily replied in a complaining manner.

"*Okay, Ok! I'm leaving in five minutes! Promise,*" I reassured her.

Click. Em hung up the phone.

I book the Uber and run to the kitchen. Dad keeps some cash and cigarettes in this "secret" drawer. I stumbled upon it about three years ago while looking for some matches. I've been taking money from it every weekend ever since. I know he knows. I've come to believe it's his way of showing me love, or maybe it's his inner guilt causing him to search for some type of instant gratification. I only see the stash go down when check week is creeping up. Same with food and supplies, which also go kind of dry. I've gotten into the habit of embezzling toilet paper, mayo packs, and soap. The main necessities. Sometimes I'll "shop" for a little more if I feel like it. It depends on the day and the struggle.

Uber has arrived.

"*Later!*" I yelled at him.

No reply, just a nod. Nice, I got an acknowledgment today.

I pulled up to Em's place. They were both waiting by the window. I walked in.

"*What are you, both my pets? Waiting by the window all night?*" I shouted.

"*Shutter down. Let's go see Jax for the stuff and pick up some booze. It's getting late, and I am still sober. Absolute nonsense! Let's go!*" She snarls back with her horrible fake British accent and pushes us out the door.

We arrive at Jax's place. Of course, there are dopey, thirsty, and half-naked 18-year-old girls hanging about. To be fair, I doubt Jax could hold up a proper conversation with a well-grounded and mature female. Just picturing the scene is a total delight with a dab of cringe.

"*Hey, Jax! Hey, drug feins!*" Emily jokingly says

The girls awkwardly laugh and say hi, slightly embarrassed by the truth of it.

"*What's up, ladies? What's poppin'?*" Jax happily yells, wearing a ridiculous jumpsuit.

I looked at Em and Lilly; we didn't have to say anything to understand that we were all silently laughing at this poor dude. I'm still surprised he no longer lives in his grandmother's basement. Truthfully, he would be better off by the looks of his apartment. How can one make so much money yet live in such conditions? Every time I question this, I remind myself that some things are simply better left unknown.

Jax brings us down the hall to his "shop," as he likes to call it, where the door has five heavy-duty locks. Scrambling through his keys while we awkwardly wait in silence, I can feel the eerie vibes from this place making Lilly uneasy.

Finally, we enter. I was surprised at how nice and clean the shop was, as the rest of his place was the complete opposite. I can tell Lilly is aching to get out of here. She has been so fidgety you would almost think she had a twitching problem. I nudge Em and give her a head nod to insinuate that we should get the stuff and kick rocks. Em asks for weed, coke, and some MDMA. I haven't done MDMA yet, and Em claims it's the best feeling in the world. Maybe I will try some tonight at the rave if the vibe is right. We exchange the money for the drugs and leave Jax's trap house. Now it's time to pick up the booze, which we let Lilly decide on since she won't be doing any of the fun stuff with us. Of course, she goes straight for the fireball; Em rolls her eyes.

"*Again, with that shit! What are you, 80 years old, going on 15 now?*" Emily sneered.

"*Shut up, Em; it's the only hard liquor I can bear to drink; everything else tastes so bad,*" Lilly bites back.

"*At least our breath will smell nice!*" I add jokingly, trying to get Em off Lil's case.

I've always been the mediator for the group. Em and Lilly are so different, and I, well, I'm sort of a hybrid. I usually just go with the flow. Emily can be very extraverted and direct. Meanwhile, Lilly is much more reserved and will wait until she is at her wit's end to blow up. But we make it work; we're a good little trio.

We were passing the bottle back and forth, taking swigs as we walked towards the rave. Lilly was already drunk. She’s a lightweight. It doesn’t take her much to get "Lola" out. Lola is her alter ego. She does not make an appearance that often, but when she does, it’s always one for the books.

CHAPTER 3

BEWITCHED

I could hear the bass of the music slowly getting louder as we approached our destination. There was something about the low frequencies that made the cells in my body tingle. My soul drifted into these vibrations, feeling them move through each cell, atom, or neuron in every single part of me.

My entire mind, body, and soul got lost in a world where no one and nothing could hurt me. If only doctors could prescribe a dose of bass to clear the bad energies, that would be revolutionary. The Bass Doctor—now that's also a great DJ name.

We danced our way to the line-up, which seemed excessively long. I mean, it made sense considering the main event that night was Alix Perez, a true legend in the world of bass.

"What a ridiculous line-up! At least we still have half of the fireball left to finish before we get in. Time to get lit!" Em yells as we line up.

Everybody else in line joined in to cheer and dance to the echoes of the music coming from the venue. That was one thing I loved about that community. Everyone leaves judgment at the door and becomes your friend. So, the line-up was always a good time, even if we were waiting. It wasn't like we could easily make conversation indoors when the music was blaring in our ears, slowly chipping away at each ear's hair follicles.

Finally, we made it into the rave by 11 p.m. We polished off the whole bottle of Fireball while waiting in line, so Lola was out and ready to party. She took hold of my hand; I grabbed Em's, and we made our way into the crowd. We always tried to slither our way to the front, where all the fun and action happened.

Back in the day, we would insist on standing right in front of the speakers to feel the bass. But in time, we discovered that it was not worth the long-lasting earring that remained afterward. The venue is packed. Everyone is looking so happy and free that I can't help but smile. As the music starts to enter my body from all angles, I close my eyes and travel to my favourite sacred place. My body swayed with the motions of the sounds, temporarily erasing all the pain and darkness while releasing all negative energies.

Em tapped on my shoulder, bringing me back to reality. She took out her cigarettes, insinuating a smoke break.

I could use some fresh air and take a break from inhaling everyone's drug-enhanced body odour, I thought to myself.

We stepped out, and Em handed me a smoke. I lit hers, then mine. Lilly was just there for support, as she never had or would smoke a cigarette. We were chatting with everyone outside—well, the girls were anyway; I tend to lose myself in people-watching. That's when I noticed him for the first time, sitting on the curb by himself, smoking a joint, and I could not tell if he was there with friends or alone.

There was something intriguing about him. As usual, I got lost in my head, trying to assess him with my own assumptions, but I couldn't seem to come up with anything.

Our eyes caught each other's gaze. I awkwardly looked away, feeling my cheeks blush a little. I always had a hard time keeping eye contact. The moment I locked eyes with someone, something inside set off panic mode. That sort of anxious feeling often appeared as part of me felt like if I let them stare too long, they might gain access to this darkness that hid inside of me. Vulnerability has always been somewhat of an enemy of mine; my motto is the less they know, the better. I built up the courage and shyly looked back at him again to notice his eyes were still sealed on me, but this time I did not look away. An unsettling yet curious feeling arose. I offered him a slight smile, which he returned with a nod. Who was that mysterious young man? Something in me wanted to know more, yet another part of me was telling me to stay away. He flicked the end of his joint, stood up, and made his way inside, all while keeping eye contact with me.

"*Who was that?*" Em noticed.

"*No clue. I saw him when we came out, and he's been ogling at me since,*" I replied.

"*Huh, that's cute, I guess,*" she said in a mocking tone.

"*Can we go back in now? I'm bored, and it's cold out,*" Lil complained.

We made our way back into the rave.

I caught myself endlessly searching for that mystery guy; my curiosity to know more was fizzing in my head, though I couldn't seem to locate him. *Oh well.* We glided our way back to the front as it was almost time for Alix Perez's set. Alix began his set with his tune "*Untitled Malware*," one of my absolute. It's time to get lost in the vortex of bass once again. My eyes shut, my body followed the rhythm, and my feet began to move as the music made love to my ears and tickled my brain. Em was off in her world. Her head was bouncing all over the place. Lil was dancing a little, trying to fit in and keep up. She had always been awkward at those events, but kudos to her for still trying and showing up.

Suddenly, I felt someone tapping on my shoulder. It was him. He smiled, and I smiled back while continuing to dance. He followed my lead and started vibing with me on the dancefloor. We kept glancing at each other. After a while, he leaned in and asked me for my name.

"*I'm Skye! What's your name?*" I asked.

"*AJ!*" he replied.

"*Nice to meet you, AJ,*" I said back while giving him a quick, awkward hug.

The music was so loud that we were mostly lip-reading, so we went back to dancing and smirking at each other. I felt him getting closer to me as we continued to move our feet to the sound of the music. His shoulder brushed mine, and I could feel this electricity between us, but I played it cool. I turned to look at the girls, and Em rolled her eyes at me while Lil gave me her approval with a wink.

Em was always weird about me meeting new people. I guess you can say we had somewhat built a codependent friendship. I had known her since I was 6 years old, so we had grown a strong bond. I'm pretty much the only one who knew how to deal with her chaotic ways. I had issues with boyfriends in the past, trying to juggle both to the point that friends often joked about us being in a relationship. Any new faces were a threat to her and our time spent together. It took her a while to let Lilly in, but she eventually took her under her wing. It was hard not to. Lilly had not one bad bone in her body; she was the purest soul I had ever met. Sometimes I felt like we were slowly corrupting her, but she had a strong character in a way too. She didn't fall for peer pressure; I've always looked up to her for that.

Alix finished his set, which was legendary. AJ signalled for me to follow him out of the crowd. I looked back at the girls again and pointed at him, then in the direction of the back of the room. Em signals *no* and grabs Lilly by the arm, asking her to stay by her side. I shrugged, smiled, and proceeded to follow AJ to the back.

Once we had managed our way out, the music was still too loud for us to have a proper conversation, so we made our way to the smoking area outside.

"*You smoke weed?*" he asked.

"*Yes, I do MaryJane and I go way back,*" I joked.

He lights up a king-size rolled joint, *my type of a guy,* I thought to myself.

"*So, Skye, tell me about yourself,*" he said while puffing the joint to get it going.

"*Um, well, what do you want to know? Ask me questions,*" I said nervously.

I felt my heart start to beat faster as I awaited the first question.

"*If you could wish to have any superpower you wanted, what would it be?*" His question caught me off guard. I was expecting a much more personal question, but I was secretly happy not to have to go to war with my vulnerability.

"*Huh, that's your first question? Really?*" I replied with a short laugh.

He nodded and passed me the joint. I took a puff, held it in, then released the smoke.

"*Alright, well, I guess I would want to be able to fly,*" I answered him with faint uncertainty.

He noticed. "*You don't look too sure about your answer,*" he pointed out.

"*Well, you see, I would answer that I would want to wish for an unlimited amount of wishes so I could have all the superpowers possible, but I feel like that would be cheating,*" I answered with a sassy laugh.

"*Ah, humble and smart, I see. Okay, so flying would be your chosen superpower. Care to elaborate on this choice of yours?*" He curiously questioned.

"*Okay, if I were able to fly, then I wouldn't be stuck here. I could escape this hell hole and fly towards my freedom anywhere I want,*" I explained while visualizing it in my mind.

"*That's fair. I'd escape this place too if I could,*" he responded with a bit of sadness in his eyes.

There was something about him that brought this unsettling peace to me—something about the way he looked at me as if he could really see who I was. Or maybe we were both broken souls looking to feed off each other's unhealed wounds. Whatever it was, I wanted to know more, hear more, feel more, and see more. I needed to know more.

After a surprisingly comfortable moment of silence, he turned to me and requested that I ask him something in return. Nothing came to mind right away, so I sat there for a minute, trying to think of a good yet not too personal question. Something that would help feed my burning curiosity about mentally undressing this surreptitious boy.

Finally, I asked,

"*If you could trade places with anyone you wanted for 24 hours, who would you choose?*"

I figured whoever he chose would give me multiple things to learn about him, which I could then follow with the *"Why that person?"* question.

We paused for a while without breaking eye contact. I pointed at the unlit joint in between his fingers with a giggle. He realized he had forgotten about it, lit it back up, and passed it to me.

"*Damn, that's a good one. I really don't know,*" he said as he was still in deep thought.

"*Take your time; you can get back to me before the night ends,*" I reassured, appreciating how seriously he was taking this question. He took the time to think and showed intelligence and dedication—three things I've learned about him so far.

"*Were you born and raised in Vancouver?*" I asked.

"*Yep, since 1991. What about you?*" He replied with a question.

"*I was born in Montreal, but we moved out here when I was 13 years old. My dad changed careers, and they relocated him to Vancouver,*" I replied back.

"*Nice, I love Montreal! The architecture is so beautiful. When you're in the Old Montreal area, it almost feels like you are in Europe,*" AJ shared.

"*Yes, I love Le Vieux Port,*" I replied.

"*Le Vieux Port,*" AJ mimicked with his ear-breaking French accent.

I laughed, slightly embarrassed, as I was trying to show off my French to him a little.

"*So, you speak French then, Mademoiselle Skye?*" He asked in such a charming way that I felt a tingle between my legs.

"*Yeah, I went to French school for elementary and high school. I learned my English when I was a kid from playing with the youngsters on my block,*" I told him.

"*Nice. I took French classes in high school, but I skipped most of them. I kind of regret it now. I'm not going to lie. Maybe you can teach me?*" He teased.

"*I mean, it's going to cost you; time is money!*" I joked back.

We both laughed. I looked up at him to find him looking at me like no one had before, his eyes expressed desire mixed with curiosity. I had never felt so exposed in that way. I looked down and giggled shyly. He broke the silence by asking another question.

"*So do you come to these types of events often?*" He inquired.

"*Yeah, there's something about the rave community that I can't seem to find elsewhere. The love, the acceptance, the lack of judgment, and the freedom are so refreshing. Plus, music is my therapy, so combine both, and it's the perfect musical gateway,*" I shared.

"*Yeah, true. What kind of drugs do you take when you go?*" He asked.

"*I drink, smoke weed, and do some coke mostly,*" I replied.

"*Have you ever tried acid or mushrooms*?" He followed.

"*No, I haven't, but Em brought Molly for tonight. I was maybe going to try it if I felt that the vibes were right. I don't want to have a bad trip, especially not at a rave,*" I said solemnly.

"*Nah, don't try that shit if you've never tried acid yet*! *Acid is so much better, and the comedown is not as morbid as the comedown of MDMA,*" he explained.

"*What's the difference*? *I've heard that it's pretty much the same as MDMA, no*?" I asked.

"*Nah, acid is way better. The trip is a lot more spiritual. Well, I find it to be anyway. I have some with me now if you would like to try some tonight. You don't have to take a lot. Just start with a microdose. No pressure, though; I just figured since you're already thinking of trying Molly,*" he suggested.

"*What's a microdose?*" I asked. He laughed and pinched my cheek.

"*You're cute. It's literally what the word means—a small dose instead of the full dose. A microdose,*" he added.

"*Oh, I knew that I was just testing you,*" I joked, a little flustered by my naiveté.

"*Okay, sure, why not? I was going to try MDMA anyway! Plus, you claim that acid is better, so I guess I'll give you the benefit of the doubt,*" I replied, feeling a little nervous.

He pulled out this small glass vase. Inside, it was a clear liquid with a tint of gold.

"*It's in liquid form? I've never seen acid before*," I admitted.

"*Well, it comes in liquid or in tabs. Tabs are like tiny paper squares with designs on them. You put it on your tongue and let it melt. I prefer liquid form, though, because you can have more control over the dosage. Open your mouth and lift your tongue,*" he instructed.

I did as he said. He placed two little drops. The taste is somewhat bitter but not as wicked as I expected it to be. He then placed four drops under his tongue. I could feel my palms getting sweaty from the nerves. I didn't know what to expect, and now I was with that enigmatic specimen. Em had always believed that I trusted people too easily. Something felt different about him; I can't explain why, but I felt myself wanting to know more as I spent more time with him.

I fear getting close to anyone. It takes a lot for me to be interested in someone. People stink and will only disappoint you most of the time. I used to believe I was good at reading people's energy. But I have gotten myself into trouble way too many times in the past for trusting individuals too quickly.

In a weird way that I had yet to understand, I felt connected to AJ. Maybe I was desperate to feel seen or wanted. Who knows? Everything and everyone feels numb nowadays. But he made me feel something I hadn't felt before like he had cast some type of spell on me.

CHAPTER 4

WHAT IS TIME?

I began to feel the tips of my fingers tingle a little, and each breath felt more intense. AJ noticed me fidgeting and laughed while trying to look at the size of my pupils. The acid was making me feel a little anxious, so I couldn't find the courage to look back at him.

"*Is everything all right?*" He questioned.

"*Yes, all is well." I think I'm starting to feel the high. My fingers feel funny,*" I shared.

"*Should we go back inside? Maybe it will make you feel better with the music and your friends around,*" he suggested.

I did not know how I was feeling; part of me wanted to go find the girls. But another part of me was feeling nervous about being in a crowd, so maybe staying outside would be best.

"*Nah, maybe not right away. I feel like the crowd might be too much for me to handle now. Let's go for a walk and smoke a joint. I'm feeling the outdoors more, I think,*" I proposed.

He extended his arm; I swooped mine in, latched on, and off we went into the night.

We walked towards a park, where I noticed this beautiful giant tree swaying in the wind. The leaves vibrated to the echoes of the night, while the roots were grounded in the earth so deeply that they secured the tree while it slept.

"*Let's go sit by that tree,*" I pointed out. He followed. We sat. He took out another rolled joint and lit it. He took three puffs and then passed it to me. I did the same and passed it back. I held in the smoke for as long as I could until it forced me to cough it out. Everything felt like it was vibrating, and everything looked like it was vibrating. I felt myself wanting to lie down on the grass, so I listened to my instinct and did so. He joined me. The stars were so clear, flickering in the sky. It reminded me how much space and depth there are in this galaxy. I once read something that stuck with me; I can't seem to remember where, but it said:

"There are dead stars that still shine because their light is trapped in time."

As I began to get lost in thought about time, I began to see visuals of what seemed to me to be the disks of spiral galaxies.

Time—what is time? Time is merely an illusion created by the human mind to provide comfort and a sense of order. If time could be saved, every one of us would be a hoarder. The time that slips away causes regret, the time that seems far away causes doubt, and the present moment never lasts. Time. What if we lived in a world where time was nonexistent? What if we did not rule our days with time? Would humans have less anxiety? Or maybe a healthier way of living? Would the world be a different place? What if we learned to let things flow and to let our intuition guide our days? I can't help but wonder: if this were our way of being, would humans have more freedom? When you are walking in the big cities, and you take a moment to stop and observe the people frolicking on the streets, tell me, what do you see? I see a failed society with endless worries, brainwashed with this false sense of what being successful is. I see businessmen and women running around on their cellphones, their entitlement mixed in with their ego-inflating heads. I see single moms working a second job, sacrificing lost moments spent with their kids, only to serve rude and ignorant customers that belittle them. I see students hurrying to their part-time jobs, working long nights to pay for school tuition, to then spend their entire lives paying off their school debt, to end up with the regret

of their career choice three years later. We have this idea to rush ourselves to success so that when we hit our 30s, we can then be judged by what career, car, and house we have. This corrupted system, run by time, power, and money, has cursed us. In a broken society with nothing left to salvage, the damage has been anchored too deeply to be undone. They manage you; they handle you; they exploit you; they blame you, then console you, only to destroy you and lie to your face. They use time against us. They use the time to control us. They use the time to manipulate us.
Time is an illusion created to create a false sense of order for the rich and powerful.

AJ put his arm around me, which brought me out of my vortex of thoughts.

"*What were you thinking about?*" He asked.

"*Many things that are now all mushed into one, but overall, I was thinking about what time it really is?*" I shared it with him, curious about his outlook on it.

"*Time is an illusion, is what I believe,*" He replied.

I looked at him and squinted my nose while letting out a laugh. "*Of course, he would say that,*" I thought to myself.

"*What?*" He questioned after seeing my reaction.

"*Nothing; it's just that that's exactly what I was thinking too. Time was only created by us dumb humans to give us a false sense of order and comfort. Let's not forget the stress and anxiety as side effects,*" I asserted.

"*Damn, Skye, I like the way your mind thinks. It's pretty hot, not going to lie,*" he responded while squeezing me closer to his body.

I couldn't help but notice the way he smelled, as all my senses were heightened by the acid. I snug my nose into his neck and continue taking delicate whiffs of his magical scent. He smelt divine, with an intoxicating combination of woods and spices mixed in with his natural smell. His body felt so warm that I couldn't help but close my eyes and get lost in him. I felt him gently kiss the top of my head, which sent waves of colour all down my body.

I could not tell if it was the acid that was sparking this rush of electricity or if it was him, or maybe a combination of both. All I knew was whatever this was, I never wanted this feeling to dissipate. How could I ever go back to reality after this? It'll be even more depressing than it already is. He gently nudged me to get my attention.

"*How are you feeling? Care for some more drops, Mademoiselle Skye?*" He invited me to take more while holding the vile acid in front of me.

"*Sure, why not? Only two more, though. I like what I am feeling now, so I don't want to push it,"* I alleged.

"*I got you,"* he testified.

We sat up. I opened my mouth; *one drop, two drops, three drops, hey!*

"*Shit, sorry, Skye! The third one snuck out. I swear, I did not mean to give you three,"* AJ gulped.

I could tell he was being sincere by the look on his face. He genuinely looked like he felt bad.

"*That's ok. Que sera, sera,*" I replied, trying to reassure him, hoping it wouldn't intensify my high too much.

He proceeded to drop three drops in his mouth, closed the vile, and put it back in his pocket.

We continued to cuddle and talk about all sorts of random things, and then I felt the acid hit me all at once. As AJ was telling me a story, I was having trouble keeping up, and everything felt like it was vibrating, both visually and in my ears. I started to take deep breaths, trying to ground myself, as the high was getting very intense. He noticed and seemed like he was starting to feel it more as well.

My thoughts were starting to unravel. My current perceptions seemed unfamiliar. At that very moment, I felt the whole world slow down to the point where I could hear my heart beating so loudly as if my ears were pressed against my chest. His heartbeat was dancing along with mine, creating its own swift melody. Every breath felt like a rainbow impaling my lungs while my eyes travelled through these vivid dimensions I could never imagine existed. My movements were so delayed that they conveyed the impression that I was floating through time and space. My fingers couldn't grasp what they were feeling. Everything felt so magical.

Slowly, I turned my head to my left to look at AJ. His eyes were shut, and I could notice a faint smile on his face. I steadily moved my left hand into his right hand; his grip tightened, and his eyes slowly made their appearance again. His pupils were far beyond their capacity. I wondered what mine looked like at that moment. Locked into each other's gaze, too high to speak. There was no need to say words as our energetic fields intertwined and made me feel love like I had never felt before.

For the very first moment of my entire life, I felt my soul leave my body and sway through the frequencies of this earth. A freedom I had never tasted before, a freedom I could stay in forever. Nothing mattered anymore, and nothing hurt anymore. It was just him and me. A sweet reminder that sometimes the most beautiful things are found in the quietest of places.

As we were lying there in our own little world, the wind started to get stronger as the cold of the night caught up to us. AJ offered for us to go back to his place. I was still buzzing and did not want to go back to my depressing hole feeling like this, so I agreed. On our walk over, he shared that he lived with two other roommates with whom he got along most of the time. One of them was from Ireland, and the other was from Ontario. They were meant to be having a little party tonight, so maybe they would still be awake and drinking.

I felt a little nervous meeting his roommates while being high out of my mind, but he assured me that they had done acid before and not to worry about it. I tried to play it off as if I was chill, but my anxiety was surfacing more and more the closer we got to his flat. After what felt like forever, but it was only 12 minutes total, we arrived. I could hear music and muffled voices coming from inside. I grabbed AJ by the arm and asked him to sit outside with me while I composed myself to meet all these unknown faces while being on acid for the first time with a stranger. *What am I even doing here?* I pondered with major uncertainty. But as soon as I looked into his dark, green eyes, everything around me faded; all the sounds became blurry, and nothing else mattered.

After a while, I began to feel better and less paranoid as AJ stayed by my side, running his fingers along my back. He was sweet and patient with me, which helped my anxiety dissipate a little. We finally made our way in, and sure enough, his roommates were hanging about in the living room, drinking beers and smoking weed while listening to music. I was relieved to see there weren't too many people there. I counted six heads: four guys and two girls. They welcomed us with a beer and a bong hit, which broke the ice a lot quicker than I had expected, but I was still feeling the high of the acid take over the other buzzes. AJ looked at me and signalled for us to retreat to his bedroom. I agreed as this was what I had been anticipating, feeling too high to socialize.

We stepped into his room, and I could immediately feel my body loosen up and my mind unwind. I let myself collapse on AJ's bed, breathed in as deeply as I could, and released it with such force that I felt slightly embarrassed by the noise it made. AJ collapsed beside me and copied my actions, which then ended with an outburst of uncontrollable laughter. I was beginning to feel like I was regaining control of my mind, all while still feeling euphoric and giggly. I could hear my cellphone ringing repeatedly, and I knew it was the girls, but I refused to answer. I was enjoying this moment with him. I knew I'd get an earful afterwards, but it was worth it.

I turned to my side to face AJ, who was already facing me, inspecting the details of my physical form. I did not shy away this time. I reciprocated and began to observe the characteristics of his facial features. My gaze lingered on the finer details, and I was captivated by the sight.

His dark eyes were filled with mystery and sadness, yet they were comforting at the same time. Sad eyes filled with despair, far too wise for their years, heavy with stories, I catch his stare, tormented by unspoken grief. His eyes were enveloped by a thick set of beautiful and dark brows that would caress the heaviness of his glare and expressions. His hair was short, black, and messy, and I could not picture it any other way as I felt like it reflected who he was. His skin was tanned and smooth, and he also had a beauty mark on the left side of his lower lip. His lips were beautifully sculpted and full, along with a slight pout, which gave his face a delicate yet alluring balance. Lips I could picture pressing mine against for as long as I could—lips I had always dreamed of tasting. He had a smile that could capture anyone's attention; I could feel my knees buckle every time he graced me with one. A perfect smile.

We lay in silence, only speaking with our eyes and touch as he caressed my skin, sending a rush of tingles through my entire body. Millions of mini mountains form on my skin, embracing the sensation and softness. He began giving gentle kisses on the crown of my head while running his fingers along my torso, running them up and down. My nose was burrowed in his neck, confirming that he could feel my breathing getting heavier as he moved his fingers along my body. His lips made their way to my neck, pressing lightly while sending out motions of heat with every gracious breath he took. He then trailed down near my chest, and his hands found their way under my shirt, gently massaging my breasts under my bra. I could feel my body tense up, and my depths became wet and warm, embracing every sensation.

He savoured every moment, knowing that his actions were creating some of the most beautiful music that two strangers could create. Our physical senses were heightened, and the connection between us was electric and magical. I could feel him wanting to explore my entire body with his touch, an expert navigator upon unknown waters, yearning for more. His eyes revealed a hunger as if every moment of pleasure was to be savoured deeply. He removed my shirt, followed by my bra, and began to slowly run his tongue over my hardened nipples, tracing circles and giving soft kisses.

He moved along my stomach, exploring every inch for the first time. Every touch from his lips brought me to a new level of pleasure and sensation that would take my breath away. His tongue moved languidly, tracing patterns and writing invisible poems. His hands moved gently towards my hips, sliding down my skirt, leaving me with nothing but my stockings and knickers. Soft moans escaped my mouth for more as I squirmed with excitement. His lips kissed my inner thighs, torturing me with such a tease that I could not help but let out a cry of turmoiled passion, removing all the care I had about his roommates hearing us.

He slowly began to make his way to my orifice, giving it soft and delicate kisses while taking in my scent. His fingers slipped under the holes of my stockings, and that is when I felt and heard a sudden rip. He continued to tear them off my body until they were completely dismantled, then glided his fingers up to my knickers, pulled them down, and then tossed them on the floor. This turned me on immensely. I could feel my opening start to drip.

AJ's tongue finally tasted my sweet elixir, savouring every drop of pleasure that poured from my depths, and his hands moved gently, caressing my inner thighs, leaving me trembling. His exploration was so gentle yet so powerful, as though he were finding and unlocking mysteries he could not understand. The pleasure was like nothing I had felt before. It began as a gentle tingle that started deep in my core and then grew into an unstoppable wave of heat. My breath quickened, and my heart raced as the intensity rose, my muscles tensing and releasing with every powerful surge. My body grew light, lifting me higher and higher until my consciousness faded away and all that remained was pure bliss. An orgasm that sent shocks of waves throughout my entire body, feeling the vibrations escape through my thighs and feeding his mouth with my gratitude.

He removed his lips once my flood was over, then proceeded to plunge into my sacred elixir, finding his way through my tightness to a place of rapture and beautiful chaos. Merging and intertwining, his maleness and my femininity were becoming an exquisite, symbiotic dance. I felt every inch of him, thick and throbbing, pushing and pulling me along as he passionately kissed me.

The crescendo was almost unbearable, with heat and sensations of all kinds rising to the surface in a wondrous peak. He began to thrust slower, every pump feeling deeper, and moved his eyes to mine with a gaze I will forever remember. Every stroke, every breath of air, and every brush of his lips were all part of his intricate symphony that felt like it stretched out into eternity. An explosion of pleasure radiated through every inch of our bodies, sending sparks of ecstasy from our loins up to our extremities. We clung onto each other tightly as wave after wave of pleasure crashed over us, sending us into another dimension and leaving us breathless.

Together, we had reached a high plane of pleasure that neither of us could have reached alone, and in that sacred union, we were infinitely connected. I realized at that moment that something new and beautiful had been created between us—an energetic connection that ran deeper than time and space. This was a moment in my life where I felt truly alive, and this was only the beginning of our story.

We remained enlaced in each other's arms, feeling our heartbeats slow down as we somewhat regained our breaths. I watched him softly shut his eyes as his lips parted, releasing a gentle exhale while he eased into his sleep. I could feel the warmth of his body, and everything seemed right in the world at that moment. I felt as though I could stay there forever, suspended in time, secure in the knowledge that I had never felt this free before. My eyes began to weigh heavily, and I eventually joined him in dreamland.

CHAPTER 5
SUMMER DAZE

After that night, we spent every possible moment together. We became inseparable. We became each other's obsessions; we were feeding into our codependent relationship, and nothing was going to come between us. Some would say that this is true love. Others would say that this is toxic love. Em says we make her sick. She is jealous of him and the time we spend together. Lilly claims we are definitely in a toxic and codependent relationship. I do not disagree with her. I am simply content with the way we are with each other, toxic or not. He made me feel more alive than I had ever felt before. He ignited a flame in me that I refused to let die out. I was hooked on him, and he was hooked on me.

On a beautiful spring afternoon, AJ and I met up and went for a walk to witness the cherry blossoms that were flowering all over the city. This was one of my favourite times of the year, welcoming the change of season with the painting of the trees, forming blossoming pink clouds as winter disappears, and summer begins to make its slow appearance.

AJ was telling me about this music festival happening this summer and was insisting that we buy the first few tickets before the prices get too expensive. I'd never been to a festival before; I had only been to raves that would last all weekend, but I never lasted that long. I would usually wobble my way out in the first 24 hours. I had always wanted to attend a big festival; I'd seen videos and remembered getting goosebumps just by watching them online. Later that night, we bought tickets and booked our time off from work.

The next day I phoned Em and Lilly to hang out, as I had not seen them in over a week, which had never happened before. I could tell Em was feeling bitter about it, but Lilly seemed to be more understanding, claiming that AJ and I were in our honeymoon phase and that it would eventually die out. The thought of that made me sad.

We met at The London Pub on Main for happy hour, which was our go-to spot as the beer was decently priced, and we would play darts; the loser paid for the drinks. Lilly was the best out of all three, and she drank the least anyway, so the real competition was between Em and me. We were both decent darters, so it was still somewhat fair; finally, after three rounds, Emily was the one paying. We regained our seats at our table, ordered another round of drinks, and continued our earlier conversation.

"*So, what's this festival you were talking about earlier?*" Em inquires while chugging the last of her beer to make room for the new one.

"*BassShuddle, it's a newer one. It's been around for three years and has grown quickly in numbers since the first one. AJ is the one who told me about it. We bought our tickets last night,*" I informed them while looking at the Happy hour menu.

"*Oh, you bought tickets without asking us if we wanted to come?*" Em observed herself seeming offended.

"*Well, AJ bought it for me. He was the one who suggested that we go. We did it on a whim! But you are more than welcome to join us. I'm telling you now, and we only got them last night. It hasn't even been 24 hours, Em,*" I replied, feeling a little guilty but also annoyed.

"*When is it? If I am free, I will come!*" Lilly voiced her concern, trying to lighten up the tension.

"*It's the first weekend of July. You should come. It sounds like so much fun,*" I thought while waving at the waitress, trying to get her attention.

"*Perfect, I am free that weekend. I'm in!*" Lilly confirmed. We both turned to Emily, waiting for her response.

"*I'll see. I'm still not sure yet,*" she replied with a dull expression. Lilly rolled her eyes and looked back in my direction. I tried to bite my tongue and not react, but my tongue won.

"*So, if you're not sure, then why did you make such a big fuss about me already having my ticket?*" I badgered Em while still trying to be noticed by the waitress.

"*Because we always message each other for events like that, and ever since you've been with AJ, it's like we don't exist anymore,*" Emily shared in an honest way that was rare for her.

I did feel bad. She wasn't wrong. I had not been spending much time with them these days, but I did not mean for it to come off as if I'd forgotten about them. When I was with AJ, I'd lose all sense of time; we got lost in our little world, and I tended to forget about reality. Maybe it was some type of escape, but it was where I felt the safest and most at peace. But how could I explain that to them without hurting them? I felt safe and at peace with Lilly and Em, but in a different way. AJ fed my soul in a way I never thought could be possible. I knew Lilly understood, but Em had a harder time accepting the shift in our circle. I was the one who brought and kept us together, as they were complete contrasts. In time, they found a way to balance each other out, but I remained the mediator and the foundation of our friendship.

"*I'm sorry. I know I've been MIA these days. It's not purposeful. Honestly, I get lost in my bubble when I'm with him. But I should be balancing it more. You're right. Sorry,*" I fretted, feeling guilty for my lack of awareness of this.

We never let any boys get between us, nor should I be doing it then. We cheered on making amends and chanted, "*Hoes before Bros.*"

Em and Lilly both ended up getting tickets, which intensified the excitement of going to my first festival. My best friends and my boyfriend—I could not ask for a better crew. Though I did feel bad about him being stuck with three girls, especially under the influence, we tended to get a little wild and crazy together, but I was sure he would bump into his friends there anyway.

It was only one day before we left for the festival, and I was having a hard time packing as my clothes were not very festival-ish. I phoned Lilly and Em to see if they could hook me up with some festive attire, and they both agreed to bring some extra. We packed our essentials and basic clothing; AJ already had some festival clothing from his previous years of attending. Once we were done packing, we spent the rest of our night drinking beers, smoking weed, and pre-rolling joints while talking about the festival.

Lilly arrived at AJ's around 10 a.m. to pick us up. She had already gone by Em's, so we added our bags to the trunk, took our seats in the back, and off we went blasting music. We had pre-rolled almost 50 joints, so we convinced Lilly to let us light one up in the car on our way there. She finally agreed after we begged her for almost ten minutes. AJ had made a playlist of some of the DJs that would be at the festival so that we could get familiar with the artists we did not already know. He claimed that the line-up this year was "massive," as he liked to often use it as a choice of word. So far, what I was hearing was my type of vibe, so I was beginning to feel even more hyped. We danced in the car, smoking and secretly taking shots of vodka in the water bottle Em had brought along. Lilly eventually figured us out once the smell got too strong, but by that time, we had drunk the entire bottle, and we were vibing.

After two hours of driving, we arrived at our destination, put up our tents, and built our little home setup for the weekend. Everyone arriving at the festival was blasting music, greeting fellow mates, and having a ball already. The energy was immaculate. I was smiling from ear to ear, which is a rare sight for people to see. I caught AJ taking in my festival innocence. He smiled, walked towards me, pulled me in, and hugged me tight.

"*I'm really glad you are here with me,*" he whispered in my ear while nibbling it.

"*Me too,*" I replied while closing my eyes and taking in his silly affection.

"*Oh, get a room!*" Em yelled at us while throwing the empty vodka water bottle at my head.

"*Let's go walk around!*" Lilly exclaimed.

We packed some drinks, some joints, and water for hydration. On our way, we ventured into the SpassShuddle Music Festival. So many beautiful people dressed up and wore costumes, along with incredible makeup. I was in awe of how free and loving the people were; it was like a giant playground for adults to unleash their inner child or inner freak, and I loved it. I felt underdressed, but luckily enough, there were people with tents selling outfits, accessories, and all sorts of crazy things. We were in another world, and I could not get enough. I purchased some clothing and accessories as we walked around, observing all the beautiful things available to us. We had already met so many wonderful and charismatic people. How did I not know about this before?

As the daylight shone away, we wandered back to our camping area to eat some food and gear up for the first big night. Music was playing from every corner, and people were already drunk and hyped up for the night. We put on our outfits. I was quite satisfied with my new purchases, and it made me feel like I fit in more. AJ disappeared into our tent for a while and then came back out with the party favours and some tequila. He pulled out his little case, which was separated into compartments, and had his drugs placed in each. We were sitting on our camping chairs, drinking beers. He finally joined us and began to announce the menu of party favours that were at our disposal.

"*On tonight's menu, we have Acid, Mushrooms, Ket, Coke, and Speed. Oh, and `Tequila!*" He declared while showing us the items as if we were on "The Price Is Right."

"*What is Ket?*" Lilly investigated while giving AJ a questionable look.

"*Ketamine!*" He exclaimed.

"*Have you ever tried it before?*" He proceeded to ask us. We all nodded a no while glancing at each other for confirmation that we were all in the same boat.

"*Great, there's a first for everything!*" He chimed in while nudging Lilly.

"*No, thank you, not for me. Isn't that horse tranquilizer or something?*" she responded, looking uneasy and brushing him away. AJ ignored her question.

"*I'm keen to try!*" Em blurted it out after choking on her beer from chugging it too quickly.

"*What about you, Skye Baby?*" AJ turned to me and inquired.

"*If I do it, you have to do it with me, Skye!*" Em yelled at me while giving me a threatening look.

"*Fine, yeah. I'll try*," I responded while rolling my eyes at her.

I was easily susceptible to peer pressure, but I had always been wary of trying Ket. I had witnessed many K-Holes at raves, and it was not a pretty site. Most people looked zonked, as if they were about to pass out right then and there. I never really understood the fun of it, especially while in public places.

"*I want to do a microdose, though, because I don't want to end up in a K-Hole,*" I declared, looking at AJ for some type of comfort on the subject.

"*How about if I mix it up with coke? Like that, the cocaine will make you feel awake, and you can still feel the effects of the ketamine?*" AJ offered.

"*Shouldn't you get the drugs tested before doing them? I saw a drug testing booth while we were exploring earlier*," Lilly suggested.

I thought that was a great idea and knew it would put my mind at ease about trying it. AJ offered to jog there quickly and come back with the results. We waited at the campsite while we continued to drink and chat. AJ returned with a piece of paper in one hand and his case in the other. He did not seem phased, which I guessed was a good sign.

"*Ok, so here is the deal,*" he started.

"*So, the drugs are pretty decent. I mean, there is a little bit of Fentanyl mixed with it, but not enough for it to kill us, as the tester explained*," AJ shared with us.

"*What do you mean, not enough to kill us? Why is there Fentanyl in there anyway?*" Em asked, bewildered.

"*Almost all drugs contain Fentanyl nowadays. That is what they explained to me. They said it's very rare that they see clean drugs. That's why they have more security and medical setups, as every year it gets worse. It's not like what it was back in our parent's days, unfortunately*," AJ replied, trying to calm our worries with some new knowledge.

"*They actually said it was fine for us to do it?*" I questioned with concern, feeling still unsure.

"If there is a fatal amount, they keep the drugs and refuse to return them for your and others' safety in case you decide to sell them." So, yeah, it's all good, Skye Baby," he confirmed while smiling at me.

"*All right then, I trust you*," I replied while glancing at Em, who followed with a nod.

"*You guys are nuts*," Lilly added while shaking her head at us.

We made our way to the first stage. The sun was setting as the night started to become more alive with all the beautiful lights, lasers, colours, and everybody's creativity; it was quite a beautiful site to take in. We found a spot on a bench by the stage. It was a perfect area to prep our drugs and get the party going.

AJ pulled out his case and a mini mirror that had a residue of white powder on it. He then removed the baggies from their compartments and broke apart the rocks with his lighter. He first sprinkled some cocaine, then ketamine, and mixed it all up. He divided the powder into three separate lines. He made his bigger since he was more experienced, but our lines were still somewhat big, which did worry me a little. We had collected mini paper straws at the harm reduction booth on our way in, so we took those out, and each did our line. AJ suggested that we stay on our feet while dancing so that we don't get too "*wonked*" from the ketamine since it was both our first time. We started dancing to the music, and I could begin to feel my body moving slowly and heavily in a weird way. I felt myself follow the flow of the sound, and I began to move in ways I had never moved before. At that moment, I felt great.

Suddenly, the feeling began to intensify, my vision started to blur, and my body felt like apple sauce. I turned to AJ for reassurance, but everything was so warped that my eyes could not locate him. I then felt someone's arm swoop underneath me for support and gently sit me on the ground. The music and voices were muffled with a slight ring, but I could recognize Lilly's voice trying to comfort me. Though I could not hear her words, the sound did bring warmth to my ears.

Everything around me was spinning; therefore, I proceeded to grip her arm with the intention of never letting go. I could feel my mouth bathing in my saliva, signaling that I was soon going to spew. I was not wrong; I did indeed spew, a lot, while Lilly was holding my hair back and trying to hide me from total embarrassment. After what felt like forever, I began to regain consciousness and control of my mind, though I was still feeling a little lost. Lilly gave me some water to drink and stayed by my side, patting my back as I slowly started to feel like myself again. This was one of the worst feelings I had ever experienced. K-holing is harrowing. *Never again*, I thought to myself.

"*Where is AJ?*" I inquired, looking around for him and wiping my mouth.

"*I don't know. He and Emily went to get some air because they were also way too high off that line. You guys should have done half of what you did or none at all, to be honest,*" Lilly badgered me while giving me the disappointed mom look.

"*I had no idea it would hit this hard. If not, I wouldn't have done that line, I swear!*" I admitted being embarrassed by my state.

"*Let's go find dumb and dumber before they get themselves more lost in the Ketamine world,*" Lilly suggested.

She helped me get on my feet, and we began walking around searching for them. Em was wearing a flashy attire, so I figured it would be easier to spot her than AJ, but then again, we are at a festival where everyone is wearing flashy things. After 20 minutes of searching, we found them both by the water, lying in the grass, clearly still on a ketamine trip. It looked like they had done more than that one line since I was already somewhat sober and they we're still on another planet.

"*Em, AJ! How are you feeling?*" Lilly asked, looking slightly worried.

The words that fumbled out of their mouths were incomprehensible, and their eyes were half shut. Witnessing this was far from a delight, and I wondered if that is what I looked like moments ago when I had k-holed. I turned to Lilly, who also seemed concerned, I then took out my last water bottle, and began to pour half of it on AJ's face and the rest on Emily's while chanting their names. I requested that Lilly go refill the bottles while I waited with them to make sure they were doing okay.

Lilly returned, and we attempted to get them to drink water, but they were both so sloppy and out of it that it was nearly impossible. People were walking by; some seemed more disturbed than others, and some were completely unbothered as if this was a regular thing that occurred at these events. Eventually, they both started regaining consciousness, and we made a unanimous decision to retreat to our campsite for a proper recovery.

I microdosed everything for the rest of the festival in fear of ever feeling that way again. AJ and Emily, on the other hand, dipped in a little harder than I did and paid for it sometimes, but we still had a great time overall. I felt bad for Lilly. She was basically the Festival Mom, keeping us safe and everything in check, as she always did.

The rest of the summer is a blur. All I know is that AJ and I did a lot of drugs and partying. Though I don't remember everything, it was one of my best summers yet. I admit I haven't spent much time with the girls since the festival, but we still text in our group chat and catch up. Em came to some of the parties with us, but Lilly didn't.

I've been staying at AJ's all summer; I have not slept at home for about three months now. The only time I went back was to retrieve some of my things that are now beginning to pile up in AJ's closet. My dad asked me once where I'd been, and that was after the first two weeks.

Since then, he's said "*Hi*" to me when I swing by quickly, but that's about it. I wondered sometimes if he missed me at all or if I was just another speck of dust floating around with no purpose. Every time I went there, the house got dirtier and smelled like rotten food mixed with mould. One day, I stood in the kitchen observing him while waiting for AJ to pick me up, and it finally dawned on me: it's not me he's given up on; it's life itself, and I am just part of it, unfortunately. It was at that moment that I somewhat made peace with the lack of love I received from my father.

As I stand here trying to heal my broken heart, I see so much sadness and regret so far apart.
My father gave up on life and love so long ago, and try as I might, my father still would not show.
Deep down, I know what caused him to hide—a life of sadness, loss, and regret since Mom died.
His love for me drained away with time until nothing was left to call mine.
That day, I said Goodbye to the man who should have been there, estranged from me without a care.
He took with him a love that is long forgotten and left me, his daughter, to remain broken.

My phone vibrated, and I saw that it was AJ letting me know he was out front waiting for me. I walked over to my father, who was sitting in his recliner. He looked up at me, confused, as I had not been physically close to him like this in years. I hugged him and held him for a while; he did not reciprocate, but I expected it. I could only imagine how much disorientation this must have brought to his energy, but I am okay with it. I eventually stood straight and observed his post-reaction.

"*What was that for?*" he questioned with annoyance, but I could hear a crack in his voice.

"*I don't know; I just felt like it,*" I responded, feeling slightly embarrassed and almost regretting my answer instantly.

"*Okay, kiddo,*" he answered, returning his attention to the TV.

I could see his lip quivering a little and his hand covering his face as if he were trying to hide it. That was my queue; it would only be more torturous for him if I stayed and witnessed him feel emotions, so I said my goodbyes and joined AJ out front.

"Kiddo..." He hadn't called me that in years. As AJ and I walked back to his apartment, I replayed the scene with my dad repeatedly, feeling the little girl inside of me shine just a tad bit. I missed the grumpy old man nonetheless.

AJ could sense my sadness, so that night, he made me a promise. He promised me that if we both got a second job to save up money, we could leave this place and move together somewhere hot and sunny. He promised to always take care of me, no matter what, and to save me from the depths of this hell. I went to bed with a warm smile that night, something I had not done since I was a kid.

CHAPTER 6
TRUE COLOURS

AJ and I both lost our jobs by the end of the summer for the same reasons. Too many no-shows from partying. I was also under the illusion that we were only 1 month behind on rent, but I eventually discovered the truth. AJ had not paid rent in three months, and his roommates were not too fond of this. Especially since I was added to the equation at the beginning of the summer, but at least I cleaned up after everyone to make up for it. I got along quite well with his roommates; it was AJ they were becoming somewhat restless with.

One afternoon, while AJ was taking a nap, I had a chat with Branden, who was from Ireland. In the course of our conversation, Brendan inquired about the late rent, explaining that he had been the one covering most of it for AJ. I sincerely apologized for the month we missed and promised to return the money as soon as possible. It was at that moment that I was informed that rent had been missed for three months and not one. He noticed my facial expression suddenly change and understood that I was not aware of this. I was confused as to why AJ had kept this from me, considering I had offered on multiple occasions to help pay rent, which he refused every time.

I poured two cups of coffee and returned to his bedroom to find him awake on his phone.

"*Good, you are awake. I made some coffee*," I shared as I passed him his mug.

"*Yeah, I woke up a couple of minutes ago. Thank you, Skye Baby,*" he replied with a yawn.

I took a sip of coffee and pondered the reasons why he was keeping this from me. AJ noticed me being lost in my thoughts.

"*Is everything all right?*" He inquired while keeping his eyes locked on mine.

"*Yes, yes, sorry. Just in my head*," I responded, hoping it would end his questioning.

"*What are you thinking about?*" He asked.

"*Shit!*" I whispered to myself in my head.

"*Oh! You know, life, this and that,*" I continued with a smile.

“*Skye, Baby, talk to me,*" he asserted, knowing deep down it was more than that.

I stayed silent for a minute before opening the doors to our next conversation, feeling unsure of how he would react. I figured if I asked questions instead of assuming or accusing, maybe then I would get a proper answer.

"*I'm just trying to figure out how we will pay last month's rent and next month's rent if we both have no jobs,*" I began.

"*We are only one month late, correct?*" I continued, hoping he would tell me the truth.

AJ began to look around the room, avoiding eye contact and delaying his answer.

"*I'm not sure. I'll have to double-check with the guys,*" he finally responded.

I nodded, not dissatisfied with his answer, as there was still a chance for him to come clean, with no definitive answer given.

"*I was thinking that we should start looking for jobs since we are out of money. I don't think we can survive much longer if we don't start getting a flow of income. Do you have any ideas on where you can apply?*" I asked, trying to set goals for some reassurance.

"*Yeah, I'll start to ask around. Maybe I could work in construction with my buddy Aaron,*" he followed.

"*I will apply to restaurants in the area. Surely, I can find something,*" I interjected, feeling a bit nervous.

That evening, Brendan let me use his laptop so that I could update both AJ's and my resumes. The following day, we walked over to the library to print out some copies.

After two full days of walking around town and handing out our resumes, we figured it was a good reason to celebrate with a few drinks and weed. We scrounged up the last of the change we had and bought a 12-pack of Cariboo with a cheap bag of shake for weed. Quantity over quality.

Due to the lack of food and the stress of the day, I ended up blacking out.

I woke up to quite a surprise the next morning. AJ had fallen asleep on the floor next to his pile of vomit and an empty can of beer. I made my way to the bathroom to shower off the hangover. Once I was clean and refreshed, I made my way to the kitchen to start a pot of coffee. Brendan was sitting at the kitchen table, reading his book. I greeted him but got no answer back.

At first, I believed he had not heard me because I was focused on reading his book, but after my third attempt at chatting with him and receiving no response, I knew something was up.

"*Did I do something to upset you, Brendan?*" I inquired, feeling slightly uncomfortable.

No answer. I pulled up the chair next to him and took a seat. I repeated my question with a calm and soft tone. He sighed and finally looked up at me with disappointment in his eyes.

"*Listen, Skye. I like you. You have always been kind and respectful to me. AJ, not so much. So unfortunately, both of you need to be out by the end of this week.*" He shrugged, looking back down at his book.

"*Is it the late rent? If you give us a couple of weeks, we could figure that out and pay you back. I will talk to AJ and tell him to stop being an ass,*" I promised, knowing we had nowhere else to go.

"*Skye, last night, 230 dollars went missing from my wallet. I left my wallet in my jacket hanging at the entrance. It was there last night, but now it isn't. I know it was not you, and I know it was not Pete*," he exhaled in the defeat of the situation.

"*I know this is putting you in a tough situation, and I know how much you love AJ. But I can't handle him anymore, and this is not charity. I need you both to vacate the room by the end of this week. I'm sorry*," he sighed again as he picked up his book and made his way out of the kitchen.

"*How could AJ do this to him? To us!*" I thought to myself, feeling as betrayed as Brendan.

I barged into the bedroom and began to nudge AJ with my foot to wake him up, but that did not seem to work. I followed by pouring a glass of cold water on his face, slightly satisfied with his discontent, as I was also not the happiest with him at the moment.

"*What the fuck, Skye? What's your problem?*" AJ growled while standing up quickly from the shock.

"*What is your problem? You're a lying thief, and now because of you, we are homeless!*" I raged back, holding back my tears.

"*What do you mean homeless? You're being crazy*," he scolded while removing his wet clothing.

"*I mean, you are three months late on rent, which you lied about, and you stole 230 dollars from Brendan last night!*" I screamed, feeling annoyed by his arrogance.

"*What are you talking about? I didn't steal shit from Brendan*," he followed, seeming unsure.

"*Why don't you check your pockets then?*" I demanded.

AJ put both his hands in his front pockets and then his back pockets. He suddenly looked discombobulated as I watched his eyes widen, and his jaw drop. He slowly removed the stack of money from his back pocket and placed it on the bed.

"*Fuck! I don't remember doing that, I swear. Fuck, fuck, fuck,*" he proceeded to repeat while pacing back and forth.

"*Well, you did, and now we have to be out by the end of this week,*" I mumbled, feeling hopeless.

"*No, I'll return the money and talk with him. Don't worry, Skye Ba...,*" he said until I cut him off.

"*No, do not tell me not to worry! You have been saying that all summer, and I haven't been worrying, but maybe I should have. Look at us now! Why did you not let me pay rent with you if you were struggling? It doesn't make sense, AJ. I'd rather split the rent than end up homeless!*" I cried out while slightly sobbing.

"*Because I promised I'd take care of you, Skye, and I wanted you to save your money,*" he replied in desperation.

"*You mean the money we spent on drugs all summer? I only spent that much because I felt bad for not paying rent. If I knew that you were spending your money on useless bullshit instead of rent, I wouldn't have spent so much less on stupid drugs and partying!*" I yelled back, flabbergasted at his ignorance.

AJ left the room and took about twenty minutes to return. When he returned, I could tell by his facial expression that the bad news remained. I felt a mix of panic and denial submerge.

"*What are we going to do?*" I asked with little hope for a solution.

"*We will figure it out*," AJ replied in his monotone voice.

"*Roll a joint*," I demanded, angry and looking for a way to dim my anxiety.

With the little time we had, we spent the entire week searching for a room or an apartment to rent. Due to not having any proof of income, we're struggling to find anything. We fell upon a website that spoke about affordable living in Vancouver with SROs.

I googled what an SRO stands for and discovered that it meant Single Room Occupancy, meaning a studio-like apartment in the downtown area. The description did not sound too bad, besides being in a more violent area of downtown, but at this point, we were desperate for anything. 575/month for a couple. That was the best we could do at the moment. We sent in our application and received a phone call the very next day.

I was informed that the process could usually take up to six months, but fortunately, we fell on a day when there were some openings due to recent changes and cancellations. We instantly agreed to the offer without visiting the building and emailed the signed documents the very same day.

I was feeling skeptical about the move, but I had no other choice as I refused to return to my father's after being away for so long. I wanted to continue to live off the last moment we had; I knew the chances of it occurring again were slim. I held on to that memory every time I missed him, not that I ever admitted to anyone that I did.

I was starting to see sides of AJ I had not yet seen, and I was replaying many moments I had looked over at the time. I was noticing patterns and behaviours that I could no longer ignore. Feeling panic taking over and looking for comforting words, I sent a text in the group chat letting the girls know about my situation with the fewest details possible. But whom was I kidding? Lilly is the queen of interrogation. She will always manage to get every bit of information from you without you noticing.

We eventually ended up on a video call for an intervention, as Lilly dictated. She was frantic about the news, claiming that those buildings were giant trap houses. Em remained calmer but still seemed worried, which made me feel even more distressed. Not much bothered or worried her; therefore, if she seemed unsure about it, then maybe I was making the wrong decision. Again, my stubbornness won, and I refused to hear them out. I knew I might regret this decision, but AJ and I were in it together, and there was no way I could abandon him now.

Once they understood that I would not budge, they eventually gave up and told me if I needed anything, to give them a call. I felt a little part of me died that day when we hung up, as I had never felt so distant from my two best friends before. I knew I was slowly pushing away out of fear of judgment or rejection. If I eliminated them first, then I would not feel the pain of their distance as much. Self-sabotage was something I had mastered long ago and now came to me naturally. Everything I love I eventually damage.

That night I lay in bed, eyes facing the ceiling once again, with these intrusive thoughts. The mix of fear and infatuation brought upon me a turmoil of emotions I could not depict.

I love you, yet I fear you. I want you, yet I resist you. You love me, though you fear me. You want me, though you resist me.

Floating into the abyss of our broken hearts and souls, tangled in our invisible pains.

.

We are all searching for the same thing. We want to give love, yet we fear it. We want to be loved, yet we resist it. A foolish game that only ends with bitter tears and memories.

Lost in his gaze, mesmerized by the sound of his heartbeat and his smell, I fear how strongly I am falling for him. With every glance, my world blurs a little more until all that is left is the two of us. The kind of love I never expected to find was the kind of love I had always feared. I knew that a feeling so strong could only result in an even bigger heartbreak. My fragility could not condone this happening. That would be the last bit of my heart. Yet I could not resist.

In a world so cold, all I long for is something real and pure. But everything gets tainted the longer it resides. Nothing stays beautiful forever. Even the petals fall from the flowers and shrivel up from the lack of care.

CHAPTER 7
TEMPORARY HOME

Today is the day we move into our new room. It's the only thing we can afford now; rent in Vancouver is ridiculous. In the Downtown Eastside, you can find rooms for a much cheaper price, but it comes with the consequences of living in old, busted-up buildings. If you are one person only, it's around 375 per month, but since we were two, we had to pay 575 per month. I had always feared this famous part of Vancouver before moving here. I'd seen videos on the internet and heard friends who had visited share their experience of driving by Hastings, too afraid to walk the streets.

My first year in Vancouver, I finally got to witness it with my own eyes. I was in complete shock at how bad it was and how zombified everyone looked. People filled the sidewalks with their tents, trying to survive the winter, while others would trade things or try to get you to buy merchandise in exchange for money. There's a little market that runs daily where people in the community sell electronics, apparel, and other things. You can find the craziest gadgets there, even collectibles you forgot existed.

E Hastings Sidewalk

The Downtown Eastside Market

Mr. Weed Pants

Picture Credit: Danielle Gillard

When we arrived at our new home, there were firetrucks outside the building, and we could hear the alarm going off loudly from inside.

"*What a great way to start; not even day one, and this already,*" AJ muttered as we stood there, wondering if we should go in or wait until the alarm stopped. I noticed someone walk in with their key fob. I ran to catch the door before it shut. AJ looked at me doubtfully.

"*Well, if he just walked right in, why can't we?*" I reasoned. He shrugged and followed me in.

As we walked in, we saw two people passed out at the entrance with cracked pipes in their hands, all blackened and dirty. I glanced at AJ; he looked back at me, and we were both feeling uncomfortable.

"*We don't have any other options at the moment, Skye,*" AJ said.

"*I know, it's just... so fucked up,*" I mumbled back.

"*It's only temporary. This is the bridge to get us back on track. We can't afford anything else right now, and I don't want to live in those shelters I've heard of. Last week, someone got attacked by a guy with a machete and his face was all cut up. An you don't have much privacy either. This is the best that we can do for now until we get the fuck out of here. I promise you; I will get us out,*" he assured me.

I can feel the tears rolling down my face. My heart feels like it's about to explode. "*How did we get here?*" I thought to myself. I could see the guilt in AJ's eyes, and I didn't want him to feel like this was all on him. We both made poor decisions that got us here.

"*I know, babe, I believe you. We're in this together, and we will get out of here together,*" I whispered to him before giving him a reassuring kiss.

He wiped my tears, held me for a while, then released my face with a sigh and pointed his head towards the stairs.

We began to walk up, heading towards the front office. The stairway smelled like piss mixed with all kinds of smoke, and the stairs looked like they hadn't been cleaned in weeks. It smelled so bad that I covered my nose with my sleeve and held onto AJ's hand as we continued to walk up.

When we got to the front desk, two young people were working in a little office with no windows. I wondered how they felt about the smell and smoke they were exposed to with the lack of ventilation. They had a Dutch door that they could shut, but they kept the top half open to communicate with the residents of the building. I was surprised that there was no security at the entrance, given the violence in the area.

The young workers were on their own, there to keep approximately 60 residents safe. That was mind-blowing to me when I first received this information upon signing the contract, and it still is while I am witnessing it with my own eyes. One of them noticed us and smiled, waving for us to step closer to the door.

"*Hello! Sorry about the chaos and fire alarm. Someone set it off with their meth smoke. Anyway, who are you here to see? Can I see a piece of ID from both of you, please?*" She greeted us and held her hand out, waiting for our IDs.

"*Hi, um, my name is Skye, and this is AJ; we're supposed to move into room 216 today,*" I informed her, feeling awkward and agitated from all the weird vibes.

"*Oh, yes! We were expecting you! Welcome to The Serengeti Block. My name is Zoe, and this is Zach.*" She pointed in the direction of the guy sitting behind the computer. I noticed he was watching the security cameras.

There were about 30 viewpoints from the building, which made me feel marginally safer, considering the lack of security and staff. Zach said, "*Hi!*" and returned his focus to the cameras.

"Also, Serengeti Block? What kind of name is that?" I thought to myself. Serengeti means endless Plains. I think Endless Pains would be more fitting for a place like this. "*What an idiotic choice,*" I thought.

"*I'm going to need both your IDs to take photocopies and a $20 deposit for your room keys,*" Zoe stated.

I scrambled through my bag to find our IDs and $20 in change. 19.75 dollars, to be exact.

"*Here are our IDs and the money for the cards. I'm a quarter short, though, sorry. I'll give it to you when I get more change!*" I promised.

"*Don't worry about it. It's only a quarter. They won't even notice. Here are your room keys. If you lose them, we will take your deposit and make copies for you. If you lose them a second time, it'll be another 20 dollars for the new ones since your deposit will have been used up already. It happens way too much here,"* she informed.

"*All right, I'm guessing you guys already had a tour of the building since you signed the contracts?*" She assumed.

"*No, actually, we signed them via email without visiting the place. We were kind of desperate for anything, as we had to move in somewhere as soon as possible. With the rent prices now, we couldn't afford anything else,"* AJ explained to her.

Zoe looked a little surprised by his answer. She turned towards Zach, and they both looked a little worried on our behalf. I started to wonder what we got ourselves into by moving here.

"*All right, I will show you around then. Follow me!*" She stammered.

We followed her up to the third floor, where the common room was. There were three old couches covered in stains and burn marks, which reminded me of Dad's recliner. The walls were painted a light brownish-beige colour, with graffiti and stains complementing them.

There was an old TV with a DVD player, and next to it was a box filled with DVDs in and out of the cases, all scratched up. Zoe explained that they once tried having a flat screen on the wall several months ago, but it got stolen within the first night of being there, so now everybody pays for it by having to watch half-scratched DVDs on a 2002 television.

"*Surely nobody will want to claim an old piece of garbage like that!*" Zoe exclaimed, "*But you never know here. Anything is possible,*" she followed with an uneasy chuckle.

"*Drug use or smoking is not permitted in here; we have a separate room for that. There are cameras in here as well, so we can keep an eye on overdoses and violence. Harm reduction supplies are kept here for you to always have access to. If you see that there are missing supplies, please inform us right away. No needle or pipe sharing should be happening, but that's out of our control.*"

She walked us towards a door with a sign up above it that read:

USING ROOM,
PLEASE DO NOT USE IT ALONE.
FIND YOURSELF A USING BUDDY!

I quickly glanced at AJ; I noticed he looked a little tense. I grabbed his hand and squeezed it tight, letting him know I was by his side. He squeezed my hand three times, which meant "*I Love you.*" We came up with that one night when we were cuddling in bed. That was at the very beginning when things still felt new and enchanting. I squeezed four times back, meaning, "*I Love You More.*" She opened the door and signaled for us to step in; AJ went in first, and I followed, while Zoe followed behind me. As we entered the room, I noticed one lady who looked like she could be in her 60s sitting on the floor, folded frontward to the point where her face was deep in her knees. I turned to Zoe and looked at her with worried eyes, but she laughed at my reaction.

"*That's Sharron. Don't worry about her. She always ends up in that position. I have a feeling that over the years of passing out high like that for hours on end, her body has folded in all the possible ways you could imagine. She's a tough cookie on this one. You will see for yourself. She always puts up a fight, even when there is no need,*" she jeered.

AJ and I laughed, still worried about the old gal. I mean, shouldn't she at least check on her breathing?

I saw a younger male sitting at the table, preparing his fix. Music is blaring, his head is bumping, and I can hear some faint old-school hip-hop escaping his headphones. He is so focused on his fix that he does not notice us until Zoe waves in his face for him to snap out of his bubble. He gave us a friendly smile, put down his supplies, removed his headphones and proceeded to welcome us.

"*Some new faces! Welcome, fellow roommates, residents, friends, or whatever you want to call it. I'm Spaz. If you have any questions about the people here or need any supplies, I'm your man! Room 419. I'm still waiting on room 420 to OD so I can get his room,*" he snickered.

"*Spaz! Come on, dude! No gossiping or dealing under my nose, and you must stop saying that. You're going to feel bad if it does happen one day,*" Zoe snapped back at him.

He laughed at her reaction, clearly enjoying her annoyance with his comments.

"*Chill out, Zoe. You know I'm only joking. But I know one way we can fix this situation,*" Spaz replied.

"*How is that, Spaz?*" She inquired with displeasure.

"*Switch our rooms, and I won't have to keep making that joke. I've told you this many times, but you won't listen, so I must continue this wisecrack,*" he explained.

Zoe rolled her eyes at him, turned to us, and motioned for us to leave the room. As we exited, Spaz continued to babble on about something, and Zoe shut the door behind us.

"*I would suggest keeping away from Spaz but staying on his good side at the same time. He annoyingly runs things in here, but you do not want to get too involved with him if you don't want trouble,*" she warned us.

We continued our way to the fourth floor, where the kitchen area was. We stepped in, and I noticed an old man sitting on a chair by the oven, cooking some Mr. Noodle soup. He did not seem like the others we'd met so far; he didn't appear as though he belonged in a place like this.

"*This is John, one of our kindest residents here. John, say hello to Skye and AJ! They are moving in today; I am showing them around,*" she dictated.

John waved at us and quickly returned his concentration to his soon-to-be-ready soup.

"*He doesn't belong here. He's a bit on the slow side. He's never done any drugs in his life, though. I don't know how he ended up here. He never gets any visitors, either. It's quite sad. He's very sweet and keeps to himself. I hate that he ended up here.*" She whispered loud enough for him to hear, but he did not seem to catch on.

"This is a public kitchen for all residents to use. Again, no drugs in here. It still happens, so if you see anyone using drugs, please tell the office immediately. Don't worry. It is always anonymous, so you don't have to stress about anyone holding a grudge. I would suggest not leaving your food in the public fridge, as it will be taken. But it's at your discretion. If you leave your food here, we are not responsible for it being stolen. There is a vending machine with chips and pop in the corner by the table. It only works half the time. Again, we are not responsible for the machine if it eats your money. The company comes by once a week to refill it, so you can speak with them. The kitchen is open from 9 a.m. to 8 p.m. No exceptions. Any questions?" She asked.

We both nodded. "*No,*" it was a kitchen, so it was straightforward.

"All right, well, that's about it; the building has 8 floors, and you are on the second. I will let you guys get set up in your new room. If you have any more questions or need anything we can help with, don't hesitate to come see us. Visiting hours are from 10 a.m. to 10 p.m. Your guests must sign in with their ID. We can scan it so that they do not always have to show it if they are frequent visitors. Bathrooms are communal. If you notice someone being in there for over an hour, please come tell us right away. One-

quarter of our overdoses occur there, and we must call the firefighters to come to break open the door for us. They aren't too pleased with how often this happens, as you can imagine." She shared.

"*Also, try to avoid taking the elevator. It breaks down almost every week. I once got stuck in there for almost 3 hours. It was horrible. You're on the second floor anyway, so that won't be too much of an issue for the both of you,*" she reassured us.

Restitution, Institution, Solution

Picture Credit: Rebekah BT

Edited By: Danielle Gillard

"*Oh yeah, I forgot to mention; we do room checks due to the high number of overdoses that occur here,*" she continued.

"*Room checks? What do you mean?*" AJ inquired for a better understanding.

"*We have a Point of Contact sheet we need to fill out, basically checking off the residents here as we see them throughout the day. If we do not see you by 5 p.m., we will come knocking on your door to check on you. If you do not answer, we have the right to enter your room to make sure you are safe and alive. So, if you want to avoid surprise entries, then I would suggest you come to the front desk every day. If we don't see you for 72 hours, we file a missing person report,*" she explained.

We both nodded in acknowledgement, feeling a bit weirded out by this whole process but willing to comply if that gave us a roof over our heads while figuring out a way out of there.

We thanked her and made our way to our new but temporary home.

I unlocked the door and swung it open. I was shocked at what was presented before us. The room was a lot smaller than we had anticipated, and it kind of had the vibe of a bigger prison cell. The room was cold, with a twin bed by the window. The walls were painted white, and the kitchen counter and sink were all metallic, accompanied by a mini fridge that resided under the counter.

At the entrance, there was an open closet with shelves on the right to hang and store our clothing, and that was it. 575/month, you get what you give. *This is only temporary*, I repeated to myself. I really had no idea what we were getting ourselves into. I could feel anxiety rushing through my entire body, so I proceeded to sit on the bed and take some deep breaths to calm down. AJ sat beside me and leaned his head on my shoulder. I instantly broke down in tears. I was processing all that we had seen today, realizing that this was just the surface of what we were going to be surrounded with.

"*We're nothing like them, AJ. What are we doing here?"* I cried out in a panic.

"*Skye, please calm down; I know what you mean, but what else do you want us to do? Do you want to move back in with your old man?*" He questioned.

"*No! I can't ever move back there. You know that. He probably doesn't even remember that I exist. I'd rather be in this shithole than live with that asshole,"* I scoffed.

We were both in silence for a while, filtering the images of today and feeling fainthearted. AJ pulled out a joint, lit it up, and passed it to me to take the first puffs.

"*You do the honours and baptize our new home, Skye Baby,*" he insisted.

"*At least we can smoke in here. That's probably the only thing on our side,*" I joked heavy-heartedly.

It's 8 p.m., and we are exhausted. The weed hit our brains right away. We were both lying in our new bed, trying to accept the good and the bad with equanimity. Our breaths whispered softer as we slowly fell asleep, permitting us to escape this reality just for a little while.

I woke up to the sound of people yelling in the hallway. I jumped up, ran to the door, and opened it. At about 12 meters from me lay a young unconscious female looking quite frail, and she did not seem to be doing too well.

"*Overdose! Overdose!*" A man yelled repeatedly, rushing past me.

Others gathered around the young woman, yelling her name and dampening her forehead with a wet cloth.

"*Give her a Narcan!*" A woman standing at her door yelled across the hallway.

"*We don't have any, do you?*" Another resident shouted back.

"*For fuck's sake, you're telling me you're shooting up without a Narcan kit around, you goof!*" She replied, annoyed at the ignorance of the younger residents.

"*Shut up, Rita; now is not the time for your bullshit!*" He replied.

The staff arrived with what seemed to be an oxygen tank and multiple black kits that read Naloxone on them.

"*Everyone, get out of the way and* give *her some space!*" One of the staff members yelled.

"*Have you given her any Narcan yet?*" He asked while assessing the young woman.

"*No, we didn't have any on us*," the resident replied.

"*I told them they were goofs for using without one*," Rita hollered.

"*Shut up, Rita! No one cares about what you think,*" the resident yelled back, annoyed by her insults.

"*Okay, guys, seriously, right now? Simmer down, both of you please,*" the worker instructed while putting the oxygen mask on the young girl and then got on with giving her two Narcan shots.

The other staff member was on the phone with the 911 operator, explaining the situation. They both seemed rather calm about an overdose happening, while this was our first time witnessing one. I was in shock at how careless the other residents seemed to be about the situation.

Does it happen that often that this has become the norm for them? I wondered to myself. The staff attending to the young girl dictated to the other worker to inform the operator that he had now given her 0.8mg of naloxone and had the oxygen mask on her. The young girl seemed to slowly regain consciousness as the paramedics made their way to the scene. The workers stood away from the girl to give her space for them to continue working on her, giving her a third Narcan shot. They checked her pupils with a flashlight, then turned her to her side, and she began breathing again.

"*Hello, miss, can you tell me your name?*" One of them asked her.

"*Jen, Jenna*," She mumbled back, trying to catch her breath.

"*Hi Jenna, my name is Nicole, and we were called here because you just had an overdose. Are you aware that this happened, Jenna?*" She asked her.

"*No, I was trying to get to the bathroom*," she mumbled again while fidgeting on the floor.

"*Did you guys Narcan me?*" She cried out when she realized she felt sober and sick.

"*Yes, the staff gave you two shots, and we gave you one just to be sure*," she confirmed with her.

"*What the fuck! I didn't need three shots of Narcan, you idiots!*" The young girl replied angrily.

I could not understand why she would be so upset, considering she might not still be here if it weren't for the staff reacting quickly. *What is this place*? *How are people so ruthless*?

"*Well, Jenna, if we didn't do so, you might not still be here, able to yell at us right now,*" the other paramedic replied with a slight laugh, trying to de-escalate the situation.

"*Well, now I have to go find more money for drugs, thanks to you assholes*," she fumed.

"*I'm sorry you feel angry, Jenna. Would you like to go to the hospital just to make sure that everything is okay? If nobody saw you fall, you might have hit your head hard and have a concussion*," replied the paramedic with the annoyance of her arrogance.

"*You're all fucking concussions, and I won't go to the hospital*," she grunted as she sat herself up on the wall.

"*Alright, Jenna, we won't force you*," confirmed the woman.

The staff and the paramedics looked at each other and laughed while shrugging it off. The paramedics packed up their stuff, and the staff returned the oxygen to the office and returned to their duties.

AJ shut the door, and we both stared at each other in total confusion about what had just happened outside of our room.

"*What the fuck was that?*" He exclaimed, holding his hands on his head.

"*Honestly, I am flabbergasted. I have no words. She got upset at them for saving her life!*" I breathed.

"*The staff and paramedics did not even seem to be phased by that at all*," he added.

"*Right! It didn't seem like their first time hearing that, either. That's so fucked*," I muttered as AJ joined me, taking a seat on the bed.

"*Want to get out of here?*" He asked, staring blankly at the wall.

"*Yeah, fucking please*," I replied.

We passed by the front desk to make our way out, and AJ stopped to talk with the staff.

"*That was nuts what they did back there!*" He said to them.

"*That happens more than we wish. We're just here handing out safe supplies and keeping you alive,*" one of them answered, looking blasé at it all.

"*Do they always get mad when you shoot them with that Narcan stuff?*" AJ asked.

"*Not always, but often. It takes away their buzz completely, and if they get more than they need, it makes them feel sick. Some of them will apologize for getting upset, and some of them won't. That's the game here*," the other staff member replied.

"*What do you guys use?*" He inquired, looking back and forth at us.

"*Uh, I mostly do cocaine, GHB, and ketamine. I also like Acid, mushrooms, MDMA, weed, and alcohol. We've never tried anything harder than that,*" AJ informed him.

"*Same, except the GHB,*" I replied shyly.

"*Huh, what are you guys doing here? What you saw today is what you will see almost every day. So, I would rethink if you really wanted to live here*," he faltered.

"*Well, we don't have any other choice right now. We don't plan on being here for long. We want to get jobs, save a bit of money, and then move to a better place. It's kind of hard to get a place with no jobs and no money in Vancouver*," AJ replied, feeling a little defeated.

"*That's fair. Rent is crazy nowadays. Well, if ever you need anything or are looking to move to a better-suited place, you should talk to Zoe. She does outreach work, and she is knowledgeable about all that stuff. If you need simpler things like food, clothes, blankets, or coffee, then hit up anyone at the front desk, and we can help you with that. My name is Chris, by the way!*" He elaborated.

"*Thanks, Chris. I'm AJ. This is Skye,*" AJ said as he pointed at me.

I waved and smiled.

"*Nice to meet you both; have a good one!*" He replied.

We went on with our day, escaping the gates of this hellhole for now.

That week, in The Serengeti Block, there were five ODs, two bloody fights, and one mini-fire from some older resident lighting paper on fire while being high and in psychosis. Nobody died, surprisingly enough.

"What is this place?" I whispered to myself.

Welcome to Hastings

Picture Credit: Rebekah BT

Edited By: Danielle Gillard

CHAPTER 8

DANCE WITH THE DEVIL

Today marks two months of living in this nightmare, and we are somewhat getting immune to the ways around here. AJ is more than me, but I am getting there. Though this place has more cons than pros, I did notice something that I did not expect. Selflessness. So much selflessness. I've never seen a community so selfless, always ready to lend a hand—a few bucks, food, weed, clothing, anything that they could help with. Except for the week before the government checks came in, by then, everyone had spent their money, used up their drugs, and eaten up all their food. Some get extremely dope sick, which then causes a paroxysm of weeping cries throughout the building, with neighbours begging for a hit and willing to exchange for anything. This was a whole other world, a community that had been failed and forgotten time after time, a community that must now suffer the wrath of it all.

We still had not managed to find work. Our physical appearance and lack of enthusiasm led to one rejection after another. It was hard to get access to the laundry room; you would have to reserve a time, and as newbies, our times would often get "*accidentally*" given away as laundry duty was run by residents from the building. At times, I would have to wash my clothes in the bathroom sink and hang them dry in our room. Sometimes, when we had interviews, I would have to show up with unwashed, noticeably wrinkled clothing. As my mom used to always say, "*You never get a second chance to make a first impression!*". This proved to be right in my case time after time, and it was the same for AJ.

Cursed by our luck, we had yet to find a way to make some income and save money. Desperate for anything, we sent an application in for financial assistance, or what we all know as welfare. This is only temporary, I repeated to myself once again. We owed a few residents money as well and did not want to tame our name this early on. Your word is all you must protect here, along with your sanity.

One month and two weeks went by, and finally, thankfully, both of our applications were accepted. Once a month, we would receive one check each for 1,021.68 dollars. Due to the wait, we would receive two months' worth of checks starting from the date our applications were accepted. The rent was 287.50 dollars each, which left us with exactly 734.18 dollars each to work with, which was not that bad considering we had free meals here. It wasn't anything gourmet, but on the harder days, it was something for us to chew on. We wanted to get internet so that we could use our busted-up iPad to watch movies or do some research, so we asked Zoe to look up cheaper internet companies, and she found us a deal at 32 dollars per month. That would be 16 dollars each, which then left us with 718.18 dollars. Next was cell phones; we both had one, but our line had been cut off from the accumulated late bills, so we escaped blindly. We opted to buy monthly cards for 25 dollars to avoid being found by the collection agency, which left us with 693.18 dollars each. We did not need much else besides this. After doing a quick mental budget session, I began to regain a little hope for us to get out of there. If we both put 300 dollars aside every month, by the end of the year, we could afford a better apartment and eventually find jobs that brought more income than welfare.

I started to feel myself getting novaturient as I pictured a better life for us, dreaming of all the possibilities I had started to give up on. I sat with Zoe in her office for a little while, coming up with a plan for AJ and me. She agreed to be responsible for holding onto the money we wanted to save to ensure that we would not spend it during a moment of poor choice. We signed contracts agreeing to the terms, only to have them broken in an emergency. I felt a flicker of joy inside of me, a feeling I had omitted long ago. AJ looked dubious but agreed to comply anyway. This is it; this is our way out. I thought to myself with a little glimmer of hope while looking at AJ. I wondered if he felt the same. His face appeared to show signs of reluctance. Maybe I was misreading him. I mean, why would he want to reside in a place like this, right? I turned my attention to Zoe and noticed her observing AJ, perhaps wondering the same questions as me. I turn my attention back to AJ.

"*Do you mind if I speak with Zoe alone? It's girl stuff you probably would rather not hear,*" I lied to him.

"*In that case, no problem,*" he answered, happy to escape the conversation.

AJ stepped out, and we both stayed silent for a minute. Zoe was scribbling notes on her paper.

"*I'm a little worried about AJ these days,*" I confided to her.

I had grown to trust Zoe, and it was not always feasible for me to put my trust in someone. It was different with her.

"*Yeah, I can tell. I have been a little concerned as well. I have seen him mingle with some of the bad people around here. Don't tell him I told you this, but I would keep an eye on him for both your safety,*" she stammered.

"*I've noticed a change in him like he's losing his light a little. I asked him if he'd tried any of the harder drugs when I hadn't been around. He swears he hasn't. I don't know what to think*," I shared, feeling bothered by it all.

"*Have you noticed any bruising on his arms or found any hidden used pipes or needles anywhere?*" Zoe questioned.

"*Not that I've noticed, no. But I will keep an eye out for signs. Something inside of me is telling me that he is not being honest about everything,*" I replied while replaying some doubtful scenarios in my head.

"*I will too. Meanwhile, you stay away from drugs and trouble, Skye. I hate that you guys are here; you both have so much potential, and I would hate to see you both end up finding comfort in this way of living. As much as I love what I do and helping people, this whole harm reduction system also has major gaps. Not enough focus on recovery. All our energy is spent trying to keep everyone safe and alive. People are burning out left, right, and center because we do not have the right tools and funds to be able to give the support needed to the community.*

We are not meant to push recovery on people, which I have mixed feelings about. I feel like if they still have a chance and are young, then why the fuck wouldn't we? Why would we enable the problem instead of helping while they still have a chance? It can be so frustrating and emotionally draining." Zoe opened up to me in a concise manner while staring out her window.

She had noticed my perspicacious ways, so we connected and trusted each other at this point. Zoe exuded benevolence and compassion, which was refreshing. Being surrounded by this hostility and sadness had really started to weigh on me.

"*Yeah, to be honest with you, I didn't realize how bad these places were. I mean, yeah, rent is cheap, but it comes at the cost of your humanity. I know I have no place here, and I partially feel guilty because someone who is in worse condition than us could be using the room instead*," I acknowledged with a dab of shame.

"*Don't say that, Skye. Everyone has equal rights to rent here, even if some are worse off. That's just the way life works. What's meant to be will be. I guess if you are both here, then there must be something you're supposed to learn throughout these harder times. Just promise me you will not give up on yourselves and get your asses out of here. You know I'm here to help as much as I can,"* Zoe persisted.

"*Thanks, Zoe; I appreciate it. Honestly, when I see that you're in the office, it always makes my day a little brighter,"* I admitted to her, feeling a little embarrassed about the cheesiness.

"Awn, thanks, Skye; it's nice to hear. Most days, I get called a cunt or a goof. So, I appreciate you and your kind words as well," she said in return with a genuine smile on her face.

I nodded, and she nodded back. I turned my heels and made my way out.

I took a great liking to Zoe; she was a person of refreshing candour. She always treated us as equals and was very soft-spoken. Some of the other workers were a little rougher, but in some way, this created a good balance. You can't be too delicate if you want to be respected here. You must hold your ground and speak the lingo a little. Zoe seemed to have caught on a little too late, as some of the residents still took advantage of her naiveté and her will to help at all costs. I can see her slowly burning out as the months go by. The ethereal beauty of her caring nature would only wear her out in time. Not everyone here could appreciate a soul of this kind, as they were too busy being on the grind for their next finds. But I could see her. I could see beneath the smile she carried on her face every day that she was slowly being weighed down by the depths of pain and sadness in this place.

I found AJ waiting for me, sitting and talking with another fellow from the building. He didn't notice me, so I stood in the corner observing their interaction, and that's when I saw the man place a baggie in AJ's hand in exchange for two $20 bills. I felt my heart break a little, realizing that my fears and worries about AJ were warranted. Stupid me, I believed we were on our way to a better life until he shattered the little hope I had left by selling his soul to the devil. I could tell it was not his first exchange by observing his calm state during the process. How long has this been going on*?* I wondered while holding back my tears. I could not let him know that I had witnessed this. I had to find a way to delicately bring up the subject so that he would not shut down or feel ashamed. He had been a bit on edge these days. I'd been feeling distant from him, so I felt like I should choose my words and timing wisely. I took a deep breath and walked toward them.

"*Hi!*" I said, interrupting their conversation.

"*Hey, are* you *all done? Everything okay?*" He asked, looking a little nervous.

"*Yep, I* just *wanted to chat about some girl hygiene stuff, you know. What about you? Is everything all right? You look a little jittery*," I speculated, looking back and forth at both.

"*Yep, all good. Shall we go up to our room?*" He proposed standing up and placing both hands in his pockets.

I nodded a slight yes, then I gave an I'm watching you smile to the lad whom I had interrupted while backing my way to the exit. He turned to him, gave him props, and followed me out the door.

We made a stop in the kitchen area to get our morning coffees. It's not the best tasting, but it does the trick. I have always had a special love for coffee. My mom drank coffee until the late hours of the afternoon. The smell reminded me of her. I began drinking coffee a couple of weeks after she passed away. One of the little joys life still brings me.

We arrived back in our cocoon; AJ's mind was elsewhere; I could tell as I watched him move with falter. I wanted to question him about the interaction with the strange resident, but I was waiting for the right moment. He placed one of his hands in his pocket, and I could see his fingers fidgeting with something.

"*What's in there?*" I asked, seeming nonchalant about it.

"*Oh, just old rolling papers,*" he replied, turning his back to me.

"*Can I see them?*" I demanded. Silence sets in for about 10 seconds.

"*Okay, I hate lying to you. I bought some side and some down*," he divulged to me nervously.

I had heard the other residents asking for side or down, but I was still not entirely sure what was what.

"*What is side, and what is down?*" I asked him, curious but also upset with him for having done that.

"*Apparently, side is an amphetamine, and down are synthetic opioids, which are nowadays mostly mixed with some fentanyl,*" he explained, looking uncertain of his answers.

"*What the fuck, AJ! Are you serious? Why would you even want to do that when you don't even seem to know exactly what it is?*" I exclaimed in fury at his ignorance.

"*Calm down, Skye. It's close to impossible to get clean drugs anymore, and there's always a mix of things in them. He said he's been selling for years, and he has the safest stuff. I'm just curious to try it once and see what the whole fuss is about*," AJ replied, trying to de-escalate my anger.

"*You're an idiot. Here I am trying to get us in a better place, and you go and buy this shit. I can't believe you. And once? It did not look like your first purchase with him, buddy*," I grunted as I turned to face the window.

"*Ok fine, I have tried it a couple of times before. Skye, let's do it together, only once. I promise I will never buy more again if we do. We always have the best highs together, so I thought it could be fun for us to experience it together*," he persisted.

AJ and I had a deal that we would always try new things together, never one without the other. Even though he broke that promise, and I did not want to do this, a part of me was feeling guilty for leaving him on his own. I felt like I was letting him down, even though I was also bitter about his lack of caring about my concerns and fears on this.

"*Give me a day to think about it, and then I will make my final decision. But until then, I don't want to hear anything about it. No convincing, no sweet talking, no guilt-tripping,*" I stated to him, trying to seem fierce and confident.

"*Get it?*" I asked. He nodded.

"*Got it?*" I followed. He nodded again, a little annoyed.

"*Good*," I ended. He rolled his eyes at me.

"*You do*n't *have to sound like a goddamn parent. I am not a child*," he grunted as he sat on the bed.

"*Sometimes you act like one*," I reciprocated with a sarcastic tone.

Though I always went with the live life on the wild side mindset, my gut was screeching for me to listen, but as per usual, I ignored it. Silencing my voice of reason as I always do best.

We got bored sitting in our dark hole, so we opted to go buy some cheap beers at the liquor store and sit in Crab Park by the water. There's a community of people who live there in their tents, and they all have impressive setups. Vancouver has always had a Tent City of a sort, but it often gets moved around by the government and police due to complaints from the citizens. Last year, when they shut down the real Tent City, everyone ended up on the sidewalks with their tents, taking up the entire space. The street sweeps had stopped over the summer after a large protest against them since the street sweepers were turning to violence and dehumanization to assess the situation.

The citizens once again were complaining, with no acknowledgement that this was due to shutting down the one place this community had to survive. That's all they can do here—survive horrible living conditions. SROs are almost worse than residing in a tent, as the conditions of the buildings are simply horrific.

Tent City has sort of relocated to Crab Park for a while now, and it seems to be somewhat stable. We came close to joining them when we were desperate for a place to live, but we found a room in The Serengeti instead. Sometimes I wonder if we would have been better off at Crab Park in a tent.

Crab Park

Picture Credit: Rebekah BT

Edited By: Danielle Gillard

When a person is dope-sick, all morality goes out the window, and they will do what they must to obtain their next fix. My mind has been on high alert for months in this type of environment. Though I have met the most selfless people here, I have also witnessed the darkest things. This is when I remind myself that I must not take sides but protect the balance of life, as I do not know their story. So even though our building is atrocious, at least I have a door we can lock.

So many people carry infections due to their living conditions and cleanliness. A lot of people have necrotizing fasciitis, otherwise known as the flesh-eating disease. This one guy in our building has it so bad that he literally has holes in his legs and bleeds everywhere in his bedroom. He gets home support three times a week, but he refuses it most of the time. He only accepts it when Zoe offers it, probably because she is easy on the eyes and genuinely caring.

I've also noticed so many people who have lost their limbs, probably from infections and frostbite from the cold of the winter. I have never dared to ask them, as I feel like it's somewhat private. I'm sure they would tell me if I did. I just would rather not hear the story; they are always so sad and depressing.

Bad posture is also big around here. A lot of people have somewhat of a slanted walk. When I noticed the number of people who had it, I decided to do some research. On the National Library of Medicine website, I read some interesting information.

"Heroin is an extremely addictive narcotic drug derived from morphine. Its continued use requires increased amounts of the drug to achieve the same effect, resulting in tolerance and addiction. This study was done in order to determine the prevalence of musculoskeletal pain and forward head posture among heroin users during their withdrawal. Regarding the number of times of withdrawal, in 16.7% of the subjects, this was their first-time withdrawal, and 83.3% of them had at least once tried to withdraw before the study but were not successful. In studying musculoskeletal pain, it was found that these people suffer from pain in different parts of their bodies. This shows the distribution of the location of pain in patients."

∴

Distribution of the pain area in the addicts

Pain location	Frequency	Percentage
Back	89	65.5
Cuff	51	57.7
Ankle	46	51.1
Foot	40	44.0
Groin	32	35.5
Thigh	27	30.0
Arm	22	24.4
Hand and wrist	19	21.1
Neck	18	20.0
Abdomen	18	20.0
Shoulder	12	13.3
Chest	12	13.3
Gluteal	8	8.8
Facial	3	3.3

https://www.ncbi.nlm.nih.gov/pmc/articles/PMC4137442/

Picture Credit: Danielle Gillard

This would maybe explain the informalities in their bodies, which I had mostly noticed on their backs. Most of their pain goes there during withdrawals. After years and years, it is bound to take a toll on your posture.

The night was breezy as we sipped our beer, sitting by the water, nestled in each other's arms. My mind was still thinking about the drugs AJ was holding, and the drunker I got, the less I feared them. I was so desperate to reconnect with him that I began to think that this could be a way for us to find each other again. If I said yes, we would do it once, have a great time, reconnect, and then never touch it again; it was only going to be a one-time thing. At least, that is what I repeated to myself to quiet down the worried voice in the back of my mind.

"*Let's try it, but it has to be tonight before I change my mind*," I declared to him while we looked out at the rippled reflection of the moon in the ocean.

"*Okay, deal*," he replied while taking a swig of beer.

"*Not here, though, in our room*," I clarified, looking at him.

"*Not here, Skye, baby. I would not ask you to try this someplace unsafe,*" AJ reassured me while passing me the bottle and landing a sloppy beer kiss on my cheek.

We drunkenly swayed our way back, singing old tunes out loud while stopping every five minutes for a quick make-out session. We were finally us again, for the first time in what seemed like a long time, but I knew this came with the consequence of doing something I was not fully okay with. As we got to the "*Getti*," what we now called The Serengeti, we made our way to the front desk so we could pick up some harm reduction gear to bring up to our room. Zach was single-staffed tonight. Chris was sick, so he left work, and they could not find a replacement. This happened more often than it should, and I could not understand how one individual was meant to keep order in a building like this. Zach looked up at us and noticed us picking around at the gear.

"*What are you two up to tonight?*" He asked while ogling our choice of accessories.

"*We're just going to take it easy and hang out in our room*," AJ replied without breaking his focus.

"*Who are you collecting the gear for?*" Zach followed, aware of our normal daily habits, which did not include this.

"*We're stocking up in case we get visitors who need harm reduction supplies*," I replied quickly enough so that AJ would not blurt out the truth. I did not want Zach to gossip to Zoe about the mischief we were about to get ourselves into.

"*Mhmmm, do you need any Narcan kits?*" He asked while giving us both a doubtful look.

"*Sure, it would probably be a good idea to have that on hand, hey!*" AJ said jokingly while winking in my direction. I was annoyed by his carelessness in front of Zach. I dreaded him finding out what we were actually up to. I could tell Zach had already caught on due to the inevitable worrisome expressions I was failing to hide.

"*If you need anything at all, you know where to find me*," he assured me while locking his eyes with mine. I nodded and pulled on AJ's arm for us to escape the awkward situation, hoping Zach wouldn't say anything to Zoe.

I liked the way she treated me as an equal, and I did not want to lose that. She was the only one who made me feel like a normal person. She saw me for me and accepted me. If she found out, she would put me in the same category as everyone else.

We ran up to our room and quickly shut the door behind us, giggling and still drunk from the booze. It felt like we were two young men planning to cause some impishness.

AJ sat at the small round table in the corner and pulled out the baggies along with the gear we had just collected. I had seen many people fix their drugs before, but we had never done it ourselves. I mean, I knew I hadn't, but AJ, I wasn't so sure anymore. I guess I was about to find out.

"*Do you know how to prep it?*" I asked curiously while watching him place everything in a certain order.

"*I've seen people do it enough times now. I kind of know the drift*," he confirmed without looking up at me. I did not reply. I kept quiet and focused on the next steps he was going to take.

He removed the cooker from its packaging, then did the same with the two needles. He followed by lighting the mini candle, then pouring the side into the cooker, adding a bit of water with the blue sterile water tube, and placing the cooker over the candle flame. We both sat there with our eyes fixated on the two elements that were soon to become one. The colour began to darken, and bubbles made their appearance as he continued to hold the cooker over the flame. Eventually, it became a brown liquid. He put the cooker down, picked up the needle, placed the mini sponge on the tip, and proceeded to take in the liquid slowly. AJ's hands were a little shaky, and I could see him struggling a bit, which brought assurance that he had not done it many times before. Once the first needle was filled, he continued to the second needle, which was now also full of the venom

I was about to taste for the very first time. I could feel my heartbeat begin to race a little as the reality of it started to settle in. AJ looked up at me, and we paused for a little while, both processing the experience we were about to share. This was the only time I could change my mind and not go through with it, but something was stopping me from saying so.

"*Take your sweater off,*" AJ ordered, breaking the silence. I followed his directions, and he did the same.

He picked up the blue tie and wrapped it around my left arm, and he waited for about ten seconds before he began tapping on my not-yet-visible veins. Eventually, they started to be more apparent, and AJ was able to locate a bigger one, tapping it a little more before going through with the procedure. He looked up at me and directed me to take a deep breath and look away. I did so, and that's when I felt the poke with the liquid entering my veins deliberately, causing me to almost instantly feel my body become mush. My head felt heavy, so I let it fall back. My vision began to blur, so I closed my eyes and disappeared into a land I had never been to before. Then it all went blank.

Goodbye, world, for now.

CHAPTER 9
BLACK OUT

It had been three days since we'd slept. I felt like I was beginning to hallucinate, or maybe I was just losing my mind. I don't remember much from these past days, only bits and pieces. Things I am still in denial of, situations I never imagined I'd be in. I was lying on the bed facing the wall. I could hear AJ and his peers talking in the background, but I could not hear what they were saying. My ears were too tired to try to depict the words coming from their mouths. Half of it was a complete slur, and the subjects of the conversation had escalated to nonsense long ago.

The stories you heard behind these walls were script-worthy. I swear I could write ten movies or more from the shit I heard in here. I have no idea how they come up with these crazy ideas, but half the time, it's worth listening to just for pure entertainment. The other day, my neighbor Patty told me that there is a "ghost" that follows her around and guides her to find stashes of money. Once, she apparently found a secret stash of $20,000 that the government was hiding behind a dumpster. She then told me that the "ghost" brought the FBI to her, and since then, they have been searching for her while she's been hiding out here. She claims the only reason she lives in this building is to never be found. I think she left out the part about being addicted to drugs and abusing the harm reduction system. She's overdosed three times this month. I could bet you that her body is so used to Naxalone that it will eventually no longer affect her. I can hear her every night talking to this "ghost." It's always the same thing. She yells for it to leave her alone swinging her broom; she then attacks her ceilings while yelling profanities for hours, and the grand final is a 30-minute cry until she falls asleep or gets high again.

I felt my mind racing. I closed my eyes to try to stabilize my thoughts. I was trying to remember more of what happened these past few days. I looked at my arms, and I noticed bruises and cuts on both, and they were still somewhat fresh. I could hear people leaving, and the room was suddenly quiet. I turned to see if AJ was still about, and there he was, sitting on the floor, head resting in his hands, swaying from side to side while whispering words to himself. All I could manage to hear was "*Get out, get out,*" and then some mumbles my ears could not catch. The room was spinning, so I closed my eyes, and suddenly I got this flashback.

AJ is running in a back alley. He is growing short of breath. He'd been running so fast that his feet had lost feeling. He'd heard three distinct thumps as all his worldly possessions fell from his pockets. First, his keys, followed by his Ziplock bag of cash, and finally, his *bag of dope he had just picked up not long ago. AJ was still new to the streets and was learning the dos and don'ts. But this time, it seemed different. I saw genuine fear in his eyes as he was running toward me. Splatters of blood on his hands, face, and shirt.*

Then my mind goes blank—a total blackout from what happened next. I opened my eyes and gazed at AJ. His head was still resting in his hands, this time he was still and no longer whispering. Something seemed different about him; it had been for a while, but today I felt real darkness in him. I coughed to try and get his attention, and as I did, I felt a sharp pain in my ribs. *What the fuck happened?* I thought to myself.

"*AJ!*" I yelled as I threw a lighter in his direction. It hits his leg, but he doesn't react. I tried again, calling his name louder this time, and he finally looked up at me.

"*Are you okay? Do you remember what happened these last few days? Why am I full of bruises and cuts? Why do my ribs hurt? Why is your face all busted up?"* I panicked while asking my million questions. AJ just stared blankly at me with no reply.

"*Hello?! Is anyone in there?*" I passively and aggressively asked.

Ten seconds of silence went by, and AJ broke down into tears. I was frozen with confusion. I had never seen AJ cry since I had known him. He was crying while hitting his forehead repeatedly. I didn't know what to do.

I wanted to hold him and tell him everything was going to be okay, but there was something heavy in me holding me back. *What happened? Why can't I remember? Why has my mind completely blocked this memory from me? Why won't AJ answer me? Why are we all bruised? What the fuck is going on?*

AJ eventually fell asleep, leaving me to simmer with empty answers to my rummaging questions. I decided to go out for a walk to clear my thoughts and get some air. As I stepped out, I could hear the chaos of the streets everywhere I turned. Feeling my crippling anxiety taking over, I walked over to a liquor store and began to explore the aisles for something cheap but strong. I could see the security keeping an eye on me, I guess that means no free booze for me today. I walked by the fireball and stopped, standing with a faint smile on my face in the nostalgia of the memories with my friends. It was always Lilly's drink of choice; Em hated it, but we drank it anyway. *Fireball will be good for the soul today,* I thought to myself. I grabbed the mickey of fireball, walked over to the counter, and pulled out my change, ready to make the purchase. The cashier stood there, still, with judging eyes and demanded my ID. I handed it over along with a snarky chuckle, slightly feeling offended by her judgment toward me. She rolled her eyes, counted my change twice, and then annoyingly let me grab hold of the Mickey. I thanked her with a sassy wink, blew her a kiss and made my way out.

I started walking on West Pender, looking for a park where I could sit and sip my drink in peace. I got to the corner of West Pender and Cambie Street and noticed a park with a large statue reading "*Victory Square.*" *That will do,* I thought to myself. I saw about twenty people hanging about; some were in a circle drinking beer, and others were shooting up by the stairs. One fellow was sitting in a tree and was yelling profanities at the by-passers; he was making no sense, but his choice of words were quite entertaining.

"*Girls with butterfly tattoos are not humans! They are witches who will suck you dry of all you have. They lay eggs in your brains and eat your hair at night! And what the fuck are you looking at, you piss face?*" He proceeded to yell at a man who noticed him yelling in the tree, almost falling as he waved his fist at the passing gentlemen.

I took a seat near the yelling man in the tree and took my first sip of fireball. The sweet cinnamon taste brought me back to the days before everything was now fucked, before I gave everything up for him.

An hour went by, and I had drunk more than half the Mickey on an empty stomach. I could feel the liquid dancing around and getting me drunker with every swoosh. The park had gotten busier, and the sun was scorching hot, so I wobbled my way over to a seat for some shade. My feet were heavy with drunkenness. Every step was a reminder of how much closer I was getting to my destination. Although my legs ached, I pushed forward, determined to make it to that seat in the shade.

I took a seat next to this old lady who was patiently waiting for the bus, clueless to the craziness happening around her. I mumbled what sounded like hello, but she did not hear or notice me.

The city was bustling with life. People were rushing around in a flurry of activity. But amid the hectic movements sat a lonely figure, unmoving in the busy street. Staring out at the passing scene with a heavy heart, I was contemplating my life, my struggles, and my choices.

I have searched for joy in life, but it seems to be lost, like an ever-distant dream. Everywhere I looked, the world was filled with people, yet I felt alone. The dense crowd seemed to be oblivious to me, sitting here drunk, too caught up in their own lives to notice. I had been sitting at the bus stop drinking by myself, thinking of the ones who sold their souls to the devil. I am astonished at the level of immaculate conception they relinquish every day and every night as we try to fight for equality. I sit here and watch others' stories unfold, joys and sorrows barely noticeable underneath their masked façade. I find myself envying those who move through life with such ease. But I also find myself feeling deep compassion for those who, like me, fight an invisible demon every day. As I watch my life pass me by, I yearn for the light that seems to have abandoned me.

The bus arrived, which snapped me out of my vortex. The old lady stepped onto the bus at such a slow rate that time seemed to freeze for a moment. I watched her make her way in and began to ponder when my time would come and if I would ever make it to her age. I am starting to fear that I won't as each day goes by. I am still stuck in this hell. *I need to get out of here,* I mumbled to myself.

I could feel my mind racing and my heart heavy, longing for answers I could not seek from him. These thoughts and bruises left an indelible impression on me.

I arrived at the *Getti* and walked up to our room; AJ was still asleep in the same position, which worried me as I wondered if he was still breathing. I rushed to him. I grabbed his face while gently shaking his head and repeating his name. His eyes finally appeared again, and I felt a heavy sense of relief, but only for a quick moment as the missing memories of the last night came racing back to me. He was in no condition to converse at this moment, so I figured I should get him to a better state so I could get some clear answers. I put his day-old coffee in a mug and heated it in the tiny, dirty microwave we bought at the market when we first moved here. I opened the cupboard looking for anything he could consume for some energy; I spotted a multigrain bar hiding behind the dried-up, rotten bread. I walked back over to AJ, handed over the bar with the coffee, and insisted on him eating a little. He was resistant at first, but he eventually gave in after five minutes of me hassling him. The bruises and cuts around his jaw caused great discomfort as he gently chewed his food. I waited until he finished everything before I made my calculated move. I could feel my palms sweating since part of me feared hearing the truth. He was all done, and that was my queue.

"*How are you feeling? How is your face?*" I asked while taking a seat on the bed.

"*Like shit. Everything hurts. My ribs hurt every time I breathe*," he grunted, trying to turn over to look at me without self-inflicting too much pain.

"*Your ribs? What do you mean?*" I inquired curiously.

He removed his shirt, threw it on the bed, and looked at me, longing for some type of comfort I could not give him. He had bruises on both sides of his ribs and a bruise on the right side of his chest. I sat there blankly, staring at them for a while before I said anything.

"*What happened?*" I asked him, and he noticed that I was slightly unbothered.

"*I can't remember. Don't you?*" He inquired while giving me a questionable look as if he were searching to see if I truly remembered or not.

"*I have been getting some flashbacks, but I don't remember much, nor do I understand how we got so busted up physically,*" I confirmed while locking my eyes on him, trying to notice any signs of discomfort. *He must remember something*, I thought to myself.

"*What's your last memory before you woke up today?*" I continued while keeping my eyes on him.

He remained quiet, looking down at his hands and tracing the lines in his palms. I waited for him to speak, but nothing left his mouth besides faint murmurs my ears could not capture.

Why is he so different? Why is he so distant? Why is he so resistant and malignant? He is shutting me out, and I am screaming for him to acknowledge me like he once did before. He gives me nothing but silence.

"*Skye, remember the night we met? You asked me that question, and I never answered it?*"

"*Yes,*" I replied calmly.

"*I have my answer now. If I could trade places with anyone in the world, I would trade with you so that I could go back to the day we met so you could avoid ever meeting me*," he shared with a shaky voice.

I felt my vision start to blur as my eyes resisted the water, but the tears won and began to slide down my cheeks, claiming their victory.

"*I am only saying that because I see what I have done to you and hate myself for it every day*," he continued, eyes still fixated on the floor.

The silence made its appearance once again, but this time I was okay with it. I could feel the hangover from the fireball creeping up as my head was throbbing and my heart felt heavy, so I lay on the bed and shut my eyes.

That did not last long. I woke up to the sound of our door opening and shutting. I opened one eye and saw AJ pacing in our room, looking quite distressed. I observed him for a while before letting him know about my consciousness. I hoped something would come up that would give me some clues or answers. I've got nothing. I turned on my back, my eyes facing the ceiling. There are no words to speak, just the sounds of both our heartbeats and his footsteps. I felt a weight at the bottom of the bed. I looked and saw AJ sitting in contemplation. His eyes finally moved in my direction, which was the most eye contact I had gotten from him in days, but something felt different. His eyes, which once comforted me, now brought fear and doubt into my heart.

Where did my love go? My conscious will not falter to watch us die. A feeling that is always fleeting, and if seeing is believing, then I no longer know what to believe in. My focus is changing and rearranging the images I dream of having. There are so many moments I falsely correct in my mind to unwind the pain that resides in me. But little do you see me anymore, and all I see is you searching for more, never satisfied with what is before you. You're looking for a void to fill with a high you will never find again, yet you've convinced yourself otherwise. This demise has been the walk towards your dying day, and for you, my love, every night I pray. Though at times I doubt the presence of God, it is all I have left to hope for. I can no longer save you, my love, my sweet immersion, my obsession. You have shunned me from the depths of you that I once knew. This poison you seek preys on the weak and desperate, and you have solely accepted it. The thoughts and questions that cling to my every move draw me back to you. Even if I try to escape, the chains of needs and desires grip me ever tighter. Every night I lay my head on my pillow, and these five words replay in my head. They have become my counting sheep. Where did my love go? Where did my love go? Where did my love go?

I could tell there was something he wanted to share with me, but it seemed to cause him a great deal of distress, so I understood it was nothing good. I remained quiet, hoping that my silence would cause him to finally break and speak, but still, nothing. I felt his hand lay on my left leg, then he rested his head on my stomach, and I could feel the warmth of his rapid breathing. I began to run my fingers through his hair and trace the features of his face with my fingertips, memorizing every detail as if there were a day that I might never see him again. His breath began to slow down, his heartbeat was back at a regular pace, and for a moment, I felt close to him again.

"*Skye?*" AJ whispered with a quivering voice.

"*Yes, my love?*" I answered softly while still massaging his head.

"*There are things that you need to know, and I am just trying to find the courage to tell you,*" AJ blubbered under his breath. I remained silent, waiting for him to continue.

"*I know I haven't been the greatest to you. I know my actions have hurt you over and over again. I am sorry for that,*" he shared. He waited for me to respond, but I did not.

"*I know that you are trying so hard for us to get out of here, and I feel like I am dragging us down instead. I feel like I am losing myself more every day. I feel like I am losing you every time I screw up. I messed up badly this time, Skye. I didn't protect you like I was supposed to,*" he continued while breaking down into tears.

My mind was racing. I was trying to remain calm. *Was I about to finally get my fallacious answers from the mysteries of my repressed memories?* I let him cry for a while, and then I kissed the top of his head, hoping it would give him the courage to tell me. When he did calm down, he sat up, and his eyes were once again fixated on his hands, tracing the lines.

"*So, I do know how and why we got bruised up*," he said while taking a big, shaky breath to then release it loudly.

"*You really don't remember anything at all?*" He questioned me in hopes of sparing me from telling the story.

"*Not really. All I have is an image of you running towards me with blood on your shirt and hands*," I shared with him, and my gaze locked on him.

"*Yeah, that did happen. After we did our shot, we ended up wandering the streets, and at first, it was great; the high was immaculate, and Skye Baby, you loved it. You wanted to do more to keep the momentum going, so we started asking around for some side. Some guy overheard us asking around and made his way towards us to help us out. I don't know why, but that night I brought all the money we had out with us in a Ziplock bag and put it in my pocket. When I took it out to buy the drugs, I was fumbling and struggling to get the money out; that's when the dude tried to steal it and run away. I ran after him, and he then tripped, so I jumped on top of him and punched him in the face until he let go of the money. That's when I began to run towards you and told you to follow as we ran away and fled from the scene*," AJ explained, looking at the cuts on his knuckles from the punches.

"*Okay, well, lesson learned: don't bring out all the money and don't flash it around.*" I shrugged, happy that the story had not gotten too bad yet.

"*But that does not explain how I got so fucked up. Did the guy give you those bruises and cuts?*" I inquired while pointing at his chest, trying to understand more of the situation.

"*No, those are from the second night*," AJ stammered while looking like he wanted to disappear.

"*The second night? How many nights have we been high like that? What day is it?*" I questioned myself, beginning to fear the worst.

"*Three nights, but you were pretty much a zombie the third night. You would take a shot and pretty much just pass out for the rest of the time. But we also did some down, and apparently, people get Benzo'd all the time on that*," AJ explained.

"*That's why everyone looks like zombies when they walk. The benzo makes the body so tired and heavy. Drugs are mixed with a lot of fentanyl and benzos these days*," He continued.

"*Maybe I should roll a joint for this next talk. I'm going to tell you things that might be hard to hear. I just want to say beforehand that I am so sorry and that I love you so fucking much, Skye. When I do tell you, please remember that.*" He lamented while holding my face in his shaky hands.

He pulled out the weed box and proceeded to roll a king-size joint. He lit the joint and passed it straight to me, which was odd as he had always loved being the one lighting it up. We smoked half the joint, and he finally began to share.

"*On the second night, we made some friends, and they invited us back over to their place. They also live in a building like ours, but even worse. When we got there, there was literal shit spread on the walls, and the residents were going off on the staff. We didn't even have to sign in as guests. We slipped right through. I didn't think it could get worse than our building, but I was wrong. We went up to Bryce's room with four other of his friends. There were three guys and one girl about our age*," he explained.

"*Bryce?*" I asked, as I did not remember anyone at all.

"*Yeah, that was the guy we met near Patricia*," he clarified. I nodded, and he continued.

"*So yeah, we started drinking, and he offered us some puffs of his bubble pipe. We were both a little hesitant at first, but we hadn't slept since the previous night, so we weren't thinking too straight already. We both took a hit, and you got so high from your hit, Skye. You were on another planet. I got fucking high as well, and we eventually both passed out. I woke up because I heard something hard drop on the floor, and that's when I saw...*" He began to cry, and then suddenly, there was a knock on the door.

Knock. Knock. Knock.

AJ and I both stared at each other and stayed silent, hoping the individual would eventually leave.

Knock. Knock. Knock.

"*Room Check! It's Zoe!*" She yelled from across the room.

"*We're fine!*" AJ yelled back.

"*Can you open the door, please? I just want to chat for a quick sec*," Zoe responded.

She sounded a little bothered.

AJ looked at me with fear; he knew Zoe, and I were close, and he was afraid that she would judge him for our situation since she was trying to help us do better.

I walked over to the door and opened it. She had the disappointed look my mom used to give me when I would do something stupid, and Zoe's look gave me the same guilty feeling.

"*What's going on, you two? Everything all right?*" She asked while looking around at our room, disappointed by the state of it and ourselves.

"*Yep, all good*," AJ replied with a cold tone while wiping his tears.

"*Haven't seen you around today, so just doing the rounds, you know. You both look a little tired; rough night?*" She assumed, looking concerned.

"*Yeah, we drank too much, it seems*," I joked as I lied.

"*AJ, are* you *all right, my dude?*" She asked him. He nodded with a quick smile.

"*All right, well, if you need anything, let me know. Skye, can you step outside for a second, please?*" She requested.

I accepted, looked back at AJ's worried eyes, and followed her out. I assured her that everything was okay as she continued to ask questions and express her concerns. She finally gave up and went about her day. She turned and gave me a smile. I could feel the humbleness of her facial expression. Zoe's smile had the power to enliven anyone who witnessed it, and today I truly needed it. When I entered the room, I found AJ sound asleep on the bed. I lay next to him and held him tight, replaying the scenes of today in my mind. All I wanted was to fall asleep. The thought of escaping this hell hole was rapturous in every way. After what seemed to be hours, my mind and eyes finally shut.

CHAPTER 10
WHAT IS FENTANYL & OPIOIDS?

We have yet to finish that conversation. Every time I try to bring it up now, he shrugs it off, saying he will tell me when the right time comes. I don't understand what he means by that, so I guess I'll have to keep waiting until he is ready, which is truly eating me up inside. From one night to another, everything changed between us. He was no longer the sweet, caring, and humorous AJ that I once knew. Even the way he looked at me was different. He had become so cold, easily irritable, and always too tired to do anything. I've also noticed that he has lost some weight, though I knew we had not been eating as well as we'd liked to. Most times, it felt as if he did not want me around, but when I'd leave to give him some space, he'd get upset and shut me out even more. The eggshells I'd been walking on had now become shards of glass, so I sat here by the sidelines like an outcast in my own supposed home. I waited for the day he cleared the path for me to make my way back and hold him in my arms, like our first night together under the stars.

It's been three weeks now, and we still haven't talked about it. I do not sleep anymore; my mind will not condone it. I search for answers, and I search my brain for any recollection or clue to give me an answer. I know AJ has been using harder drugs. I have been finding empty baggies and syringe wrappers hidden behind our bed. I pretend I do not notice for fear of pushing him away even more than I already have. I've been confiding in Zoe from time to time, and she is helping me in every way to get us out of here before I completely lose him.

One morning, while AJ was sleeping, I opted to do some research on drugs to have a better understanding. I sort of knew what side and down were, but that was the bare minimum of what AJ had explained to me that day. *Wow, Skye, you injected yourself with that shit without knowing anything about it, just for him,* I thought to myself, feeling worthless. I began my research without knowing where to start. I've heard a lot of talk about fentanyl and opioids, so I decided to type that in the search bar.

I found a paper study written by a student named Brittany Vaughan at Simon Fraser University in Vancouver. I read through it carefully, not understanding all the lingo, but I was still able to follow. I found some interesting information.

Opioids are a class of drugs that are used to treat and manage pain. Opioid use disorder is the fourth most common addiction in Canada (Government of Canada, 2022) and is the most common cause of death from drug overdose (Oldham, 2020). Currently, approximately 9.7% of Canadians over the age of 15 engage in problematic opioid use (Carrière et al., 2022). Synthetic opioids include methadone, while semi-synthetic opioids include morphine, fentanyl, and heroin. The DSM-5 criteria for opioid use disorder outline eleven items, and at least two must be present to be classified as opioid abuse. In this paper, the effects of opioid abuse on the brain and how opioids impact brain processes will be discussed. The current opioid crisis in British Columbia has prompted a public health emergency. Due to a toxic drug supply consisting of synthetic opioids such as fentanyl, overdose deaths have accounted for approximately 6.4 deaths a day (BC Coroners Service, 2022). Fentanyl has tainted other street drugs, making them extremely deadly. Abstinence is not always an option for people, and safe supply initiatives work to limit access and exposure to opioids by utilizing prescription monitoring programs (Tyndall, 2020). Opiates, including heroin and morphine, work by binding to opioid receptors, which are found in the limbic and hypothalamic areas of the brain (Breedlove, 2020) and attaching to specialized proteins called mu receptors. Furthermore, the neurobiology of opiate dependence will be outlined, along with how chronic opioid abuse alters brain chemistry. Abnormalities that produce addiction include environmental and psychological effects such as stress and situational factors (Kosten & George, 2002). Moreover, the cognitive impairments that are associated with opioid misuse will be discussed, as well as their effects on attention, memory, and learning. Over time, tolerance, dependence, and withdrawal become present, and various pharmacological methods and treatment options to manage opioid abuse will be outlined.

The DSM-5 lists certain criteria that must be present to confirm a diagnosis of opioid use disorder. At least two must be observed over a 12-month period and can include a strong desire to use opioids, larger quantities of the drug being taken, and tolerance to the drug (Centers for Disease Control and Prevention, n.d.). The physical dependence on the drug usually takes two weeks, and withdrawal symptoms can occur within 8 to 12 hours after the last use (American Addiction Centers, 2023). Synthetic opioids, including fentanyl, heroin, and methadone, activate the mu receptors in the brain and cause central nervous system and respiratory depression (Armenian et al., 2018). Mu receptors are specialized proteins that are associated with pleasure and reward areas of the brain. Fentanyl is widely used to treat severe and chronic pain, especially when less potent opioids have not been effective, and is commonly prescribed in the form of a transdermal patch. Fentanyl is 50 to 100 times stronger than morphine, has made its way into the illegal drug supply, and has become one of the most abused street drugs (*Fentanyl Drug Facts*, 2023). Typical effects of fentanyl include drowsiness, confusion, and euphoria (*Fentanyl Drug Facts*, 2023). Synthetic opioids are made in a lab and become addictive because they bind to the brain's receptors that control emotions and pain, causing the brain to adapt to the drug and creating dependence (Armenian et al., 2023). However, when opioids are used in the absence of pain, they activate reward centers in the brain, and tolerance can develop. Semisynthetic opioids are created in a lab and are derived from natural opiates (Caldbick, 2023). Oxycodone, a prescribed narcotic, is similar to morphine but almost twice as strong (*Semisynthetic Opioids*, 2016). Hydromorphone and Hydrocodone are also semisynthetic opioids that are highly addictive, and side effects include mental impairment, constipation, and respiratory depression (*Semisynthetic Opioids*, 2016).

The four types of metabotropic opioid receptors are mu, delta, kappa, and NOP (Breedlove, 2020), and they are known as G-coupled proteins. Opioid receptors are found in the limbic and hypothalamic areas and are particularly prevalent in the locus coeruleus and periaqueductal gray areas, which are involved in pain perception (Breedlove, 2020). Opioids operate by attaching to these receptors as agonists, meaning they activate certain receptors in the brain, or as antagonists, meaning they block opioids and cause no opioid effect (*Pharmacological treatment: Medication-assisted recovery, n.d.).* Examples of opioid agonists include heroin, methadone, and morphine, while antagonists include naltrexone and naloxone, which are used to reverse opioid overdoses. The mesolimbic reward system consists of dopamine pathways, which are associated with pleasure and reward (Koob, 2006). The brain's reward system is altered by the presence of opioids when signals are generated in the ventral tegmental area that causes dopamine to be released in the nucleus accumbens (Kosten & George, 2002). The brain remembers the feelings of pleasure that are produced, further causing tolerance and dependence on the drug. Opioid tolerance happens when more opioids are needed to stimulate the ventral tegmental area of brain cells to release the same amount of dopamine in the nucleus accumbens, in order to produce similar levels of pleasure (Kosten & George, 2002). The locus coeruleus is associated with withdrawal symptoms, which can be very unpleasant. Normally, noradrenaline is produced in the locus coeruleus, which is responsible for regulating blood pressure, breathing, and alertness, but when opioids link to mu receptors, they suppress the release of noradrenaline, which causes drowsiness, decreased respiration, and a decrease in blood pressure (Kosten & George, 2002). With repeated opioid use, neurons in the locus coeruleus increase their activity level, which inhibits the effects of the drug and releases a typical amount of noradrenaline (Kosten & George, 2002) regardless of the drug being present, causing the person to feel normal. Withdrawal occurs when opioids are not present to suppress this enhanced activity, resulting in excess amounts of noradrenaline being released from the neurons, causing discomforting symptoms, including anxiety, cramps, and jitters (Kosten & George, 2002). Therefore, daily drug use can help relieve these withdrawal symptoms. When opioids bind to receptors, euphoria is induced, which can cause an individual to use the drug even more.

Opioid analgesics can create side effects that can lead to cognitive impairments, despite their ability to treat and alleviate pain. One study found that opioid use disorder caused impairments in working memory (Rass et al., 2015). Moreover, heroin decreases gray matter density in the prefrontal and temporal cortical regions of chronic heroin addicts (Seif et al., 2022). Decreases in gray matter can affect decision-making abilities, emotion, and speech. This is because chronic exposure to opioids reduces the rate of neuron development in the dentate gyrus of the hippocampus (Rapeli et al., 2006). Some studies have found that opioid misuse is associated with intellectual decline, problems with executive function, and deficits in attention (Tolomeo et al., 2016). Long-term opioid use causes imbalances in dopamine transmission and can cause deterioration of the frontal brain regions over time (Tolomeo et al., 2016), impacting learning and function. Individuals who misuse opioids often struggle with problem-solving abilities and impulse control, which may increase risky behaviours (Tolomeo et al., 2016). Chronic opioid use causes cognitive impairments that may have long-term implications; therefore, treatment strategies are beneficial.

The unpleasant withdrawal symptoms associated with opioid misuse are one reason why many individuals find it difficult to stop using the drug. Withdrawal symptoms usually peak within three days of stopping the drug, and most symptoms subside within three weeks (Rapeli et al., 2006). The amygdala is involved in the withdrawal stage of opioid addiction, and emotional learning circuits become disrupted (Gregoriou et al., 2021). Buprenorphine and methadone are regularly prescribed to control and reduce withdrawal symptoms. Buprenorphine is usually used to taper off the drug and comes in the form of a tablet or patch. Suboxone is a tapering medication that is a combination of buprenorphine and naloxone and is commonly used for long-term treatment because it is effective in reducing cravings (Mosel, 2023). However, withdrawal management is not always the answer for treating opioid use disorder, and residential treatment facilities can be beneficial in providing an individual with healthy coping techniques.

2,272 people died from an overdose in BC in 2022 due to the toxic drug supply in Vancouver (Coroners' Preventative Function, 2023). Fentanyl has largely replaced opioids such as heroin and OxyContin and is the most commonly used illicit drug in Vancouver (Nolen, 2022). Safe supply programs are designed to reduce the rate of overdose by providing monitored doses of prescription opioids to participants. Moreover, BC has decriminalized small quantities of opioids to reduce the stigmatization of addiction (Duong, 2023). Harm reduction efforts, including supervised injection sites, needle exchange, and free naloxone kits, aim to not only reduce overdoses but also provide stability for drug users. Some say that if the government provides substances for people, drug use will be encouraged. However, treatment and recovery are not always available due to a lack of treatment beds. Furthermore, it is not realistic to assume that people will abstain from using opioids. Therefore, providing clean substances to be used under medical supervision is a way to limit crime and reduce overdoses. Opioid use disorder involves biological, psychological, and sociocultural components that need to be examined collectively so that prevention and treatment methods can be possible.

When I finished reading the paper, I was shocked at the gravity of all this. I mean, I clearly knew there was a drug problem here, but I did not realize how many people had passed away from an overdose. The lack of treatment centers is not helping the situation. How are we supposed to be motivated to get clean if we don't have easier access to rehab?

CHAPTER 11 ILLEGITIMI NON-CARBORUNDUM!

AJ is spiralling out; I do not recognize him anymore. He sleeps throughout the day and gets blasted at night with anything he can get his hands on. Driven by his voracity for his enemy, sometimes he stays up all night pacing the hallways, waiting for anyone generous enough to share their goods. I just sit here and watch because I know if I say anything, he will get upset. The only time I get my love back is when he wakes up, but that lasts a whole thirty minutes before his need for his next high creeps along. She has become his new lover, and I am the mistress. I wait for the little time he can devote to me before he goes running back to her. She controls him and manipulates him, but she also soothes him in ways that I cannot. He belongs to her now, and I have lost the fight. Tears roll down my face as I replay all the words we used to exchange at night.

Don't you remember how it felt when the tips of my fingers brushed your hair and the way I used to whisper songs in your ear? I would sing a million songs to you, my love, if that meant I could get you back. Now the melodies I sing no longer reach you, as you have shielded me from your heart; the echoes of my voice have bounced back every time.

It's 11:23 AM, and AJ is asleep as usual. The sun is shining for the first time this week, so I decided to go out for a walk to get some space and fresher air for my poor lungs. I walked by the office to acknowledge my and AJ's presence as I made my way out the front door. Chris was working today. I had only met him a couple of times when we first moved in, but I had not seen him in a while. The word was that he had a mental breakdown and took some time off work. I don't blame the guy. Having to deal with this chaos comes with many challenges. I bet the burnout rate for this type of work is extremely high. We caught up for a little, and he seemed different. He looked tired and desensitized to life. I feel like the more time you spend here, the more you lose your light that is being sucked away by the darkness of this place. I could feel it happening to me. The only difference is that he gets to go home, and for me, well, this is my home.

We said our goodbyes after our quick chat, and I began to walk with no destination in sight, letting my instincts guide me to wherever I would end up.

I walked by this young female who seemed to be helping people on the streets with their pets. I took a seat near her and observed the situation. I have always enjoyed people-watching. From a young age, I would try to imagine what personality and life they would have by observing their mannerisms. I noticed the woman handing out dog food to the people circling her, and she seemed to know many of them by name already. She caught me staring and waved at me with a smile. I waved back. Once all the dog food was handed out, she walked toward me and presented herself.

"*Jessy,*" she said while extending her hand for a shake.

"*Skye*," I replied while meeting her hand with mine.

"*Do you always hand out free dog food?*" I questioned.

"*Yes, I do Pet Outreach for the community here*," she explained.

"*Do you have a pet?*" She asked curiously.

"*No, I would like one, but I don't think it's the right time for me. What is Pet Outreach?*" I asked, unsure of what her work was.

"*There are about 50 buildings I visit in the area, and I help the community take care of their pets. Basically, I bring them to their vet appointments or find them a ride there, handing out food, checking up on the state of the pet's living situation, and all that fun stuff,*" she elucidated.

"*Wow, 50 buildings! Do you do all of this on your own?*" I asked, shocked by what she had just shared.

"*It's another worker and me. We are two people. Not enough for the work we've got, but we push through it as best as we can. Some days are harder than others, but I do it for the community and the animals,*" she avowed while petting a dog near her.

"*That's nice of you to devote yourself like this. Why are there only two people for so many buildings, though?*" I inquired.

"*Because of the budget, is what I was told,*" she informed me with a doubtful look.

"*I can sometimes help if you need it." It's not like I've got much to do anyway,*" I offered.

I figured maybe this would make me feel like I had some purpose in life.

We exchanged numbers, and she went on her way to save the day once again. As they say, not all heroes wear capes, and around here, I've encountered many invisible capes. Vancouver is set up to support this community like nothing I have seen before, yet the problem continues to worsen every year. I see lineups on Hastings for food donations; there are safe injection sites with nurses to care for the people; they have medical places devoted to the community; and there are communal bathrooms that are not the cleanest but better than having none. There's a place called The Carnegie Community Center on the corner of Main Street and Hastings, often referred to as the living room of the Downtown Eastside. It provides services for the community, like social, cultural, and educational activities. You can purchase delicious meals for as little as 4 dollars per plate; they have books you can read, and they even have volunteers to help you with your taxes.

I continued my walk and headed towards Crab Park. I stopped at the beer store to buy the cheapest tall can of beer I could find and then headed toward the water. I cracked open the beer, took my first sip, thanked the universe for it, and then closed my eyes to embrace the sun's rays caressing my skin. *What a day to be a day!* I thought to myself. I looked to my right and saw a young girl sitting near me, writing in a journal. It reminded me of when I used to write. I still have all my journals from the age of 11 and onwards, sitting in a box in my old man's dungeon. I missed writing. I don't know why I stopped. I always have all these thoughts, and writing them out always makes my mind feel calmer. That day, I opted to start writing again. I had to find a way to reconnect with myself. The girl noticed me watching, and I felt a little embarrassed, so to break the awkwardness, I started a conversation.

"*Perfect day for journaling. I need to get back at it, too*," I began, trying to reason why I had been staring at her.

"*Right! I find the weather often varies the way I write too. I always start with a description of the mood of the day so that when I look back, I can notice my writing patterns,*" she explained.

"*That's a cool way to look at it. What are you writing about on this sunny day, if you don't mind me asking?*" I inquired, curious about this individual.

"*Oh well, today's writing is more on the deep and dark side, even though the sun is shining*," she shared, laughing at the contradiction of her last words.

"*There is always beauty in darkness*," I said with a smile.

"*I like that; well said*," she complimented.

"*Would you like to read what I wrote today?*" She offered to hand over her book.

"*Oh no, I don't want to impose!*" I interjected, but she insisted, so I accepted.

I know you probably wouldn't understand, but I am here in the Downtown Eastside because I chose to be. It's an addiction for many people, really. Getting out of the Eastside is as hard as getting off crack or meth. Hastings is a drug in itself. People walk past us with judging eyes, but really, they are blind to the truth, given that we live in a culture that swims in addiction, some more visible than others. Society is addicted to oil, and they engage in a pursuit of the amenities and luxuries provided by oil, despite the fact that they are destroying the earth. Wars have been initiated by oil, killing many innocent lives. So, who are they to tell the addict that they shouldn't be engaging in self-destructive behaviour? In reality, it's all an escape. They are deeply related to the addict, but they choose not to acknowledge the relationship. In theory, intelligence is the destruction of indoctrinated beliefs that infect a supposed civilization, and the ignorant are the largest blemish on the face of freedom and peace.

I looked up at her in awe. *Is she really an addict? She doesn't look like one.* I pondered in silence. She read my mind.

"*Yep, I'm a crackhead, as they like to call us,*" she laughed while motioning the quotation mark on the word crackhead.

"*I could never tell; I was shocked when I read that. No worries, though. I'm right there with you. I'm not at the "crackhead" stage yet, but I'm sure living like one right now*," I shared, looking down at the ground.

"*Your writing is beautiful and very well said. It's true that humans are all addicted to one thing or another, but some have become so normalized that we no longer see them as an addiction but rather as the norm. This world is so fucked up*," I continued.

"*I know, right? At this point, I might as well rob a bank and escape somewhere beautiful to get the fuck out of here*," she joked.

"*Honestly, why the fuck not*?" I reciprocated, laughing and daydreaming about it.

I'm just so tired of being judged by society. I read this book not long ago about this guy who was previously an addict, but he got clean and proceeded to study addiction. His name is Peter Ferentzy, and he is now a research scientist for addiction. Anyway, in one of his books called "*Dealing with Addiction,*" he says something that really stuck with me. He wrote.

"*Addicts are not the only oppressed group, but they are the only remaining group deemed to benefit from degradation.*"

"*It's so true; though other oppressed groups do feel degradation, we are in an era where it is no longer okay to discriminate and shame, but for the addict, we are still living it with blind eyes and deaf ears,*" I vocalized with frustration towards the problem.

"*Amen, sister. Illegitimi non carborundum!*" She yelled, raising her first to the air.

"*What the hell does that mean?*" I replied, confused by the gibberish coming from her mouth.

"*It means, don't let the bastards grind you down in Latin. The phrase itself has no meaning in Latin and can only be mock-translated. It originated during World War II; it is attributed to British Army intelligence very early in the war,*" she carried on.

"*But we use it a lot here in the DTES for the cops and the corrupt system,*" she added with a laugh.

"*Wow, how do you know so much?*" I asked. I was quite impressed by her knowledge, even though she was a user, but who was I to judge anyway.

"*I read a lot, like pretty much all the time. It gets quite lonely out here, so I like to keep my mind busy and stay sharp. The drugs will eat away at your memory, so I guess I am trying to counteract it, as stupid as it sounds*." She chuckled, shaking her head.

"*Every little bit helps*," I agreed.

"*I never got your name,*" she noticed.

"*I'm Skye. What's yours?*" I asked in return.

"*I'm Luna. Nice to meet you, Skye. It's refreshing to have an intellectual discussion with someone around here. Do you have a cell numbe*r*?*" She inquired while pulling her cell phone out of her bag.

"*Right, I've been feeling like I'm slowly losing my mind. Everyone here seems to live in their own little world. I'm starting to lose sense of what's real and what's not*," I voiced, looking out at the water.

We exchanged numbers with plans to meet again, and I returned to the Getti once the breeze began to pick up. I wondered if AJ would be awake by the time I got back. He was.

"*Skye, Baby, did you hear the news?*" He gasped while standing up.

"*No? What news?*' I asked, nervous to hear it.

"*Chris… He OD'd today at work, and he was in the staff washroom. By the time they noticed how long he had been gone, he was already dead*," AJ explained. I stood there in shock, as I had just seen him today, and I could tell something was off. I felt guilty for not reaching out to him or checking to see if he was okay. We had a genuine camaraderie, but he never opened up much about himself. He was timider than the other staff. It made me sad to hear the news, and it also made me wonder about the support system that was accessible to them. A lot of them looked like they had become desensitized long ago. I don't blame them, but there's maybe a gap in the system if this is happening. Zoe had told me that the burnout rate for her type of work is so high, and it made me wonder if they simply hire anybody just to fill the empty seats. Just another failed system where we are all replaceable.

"*Well, I hope this will slap some sense into you a little,*" I whispered to AJ, fearing that this could happen to him.

"*It did. I don't want to go like that*," AJ responded while holding my hands.

"*Okay, so let's get better together. Please. We need to get out of here, AJ. We don't belong here*," I fretted while squeezing his hand three times. He looked up at me, squeezed back four times, and gave me a long kiss on the forehead.

"*Okay, Skye, Baby. Anything for you*," he whispered.

"*For us*," I whispered back.

"*Illegitimi non carborundum*," I followed.

"*Huh?*" AJ doubted the words I had just said. I giggled, thinking of my new friend.

"*Don't let the bastards grind you down*," I followed. We both laughed.

"*I like that. Where did you learn that?*" He asked.

"*From my new friend I met today, Luna*," I shared with a smile.

"*Ah, I see. Is that why you were gone so long?*" He followed, seeming unpleased by this.

"*Yeah, I mean, I wasn't gone that long, and you were sleeping anyway*," I replied, confused by his domineering.

"*So, you're going out making friends and leaving me here alone when you know I have a problem?*" He condemned me without looking directly at me.

"*What do you mean? You were sleeping, AJ. Am I supposed to sit in here all day while you sleep? If that's the case, then you are asking for me to sit here and rot. I hate this place. The longer I am here, the more messed up I feel. I've been sticking by you this whole time, so don't be like that.*" I panted, feeling flustered by this unfairness.

"*You said we stick by each other at all times, remember?*" He replied, attempting to guilt me into giving in as he always does.

"*Yes, but that doesn't mean I can't go out for a fucking walk and make a friend. What is wrong with you? You've never been like this with me. Where is my AJ? The real AJ?*" I cried, feeling more hopeless by the second.

"*Whatever, all is well, Skye Baby. I'll be making new friends too, don't you worry,*" he replied with a threatening tone. He got up and left the room. I fell asleep after waiting up for him, with a throbbing headache from the number of tears I cried that night.

I woke up with swollen eyes the next day after receiving a message from Jessy. She explained that she needed some assistance with handing out some dog food. AJ was still not back and was probably on another bender. Part of me was relieved to wake up alone today. His energy was becoming too heavy to be around, and I needed a break. I met up with Jessy, and we had a great time. Jessy was so devoted and genuine; it was refreshing to be around her. I really looked up to her and all that she did for the community and the animals. A true legend.

I dreaded returning to the *Getti*, so I opted to send a text to Luna and see if she was up for a smoke and a chat. To my pleasure, she was already at Crab Park and was now waiting for me with a rolled joint. I found an old book with some blank papers and a black pen at a donation shop. I threw it in my bag, and off I went to meet my friend.

I really enjoyed spending time with Luna. I gracefully listened to all the things she spoke about in such a passionate way. It reminded me of Alex. Maybe that's why I found comfort in her; she had the same mannerisms as he did. Passionate, knowledgeable, and funny. We began to meet up almost every day for a joint writing session. She became my little escape from hell. AJ was still bitter about it, but he was always asleep when I left, so I would only hear his complaints upon my return. It became the daily routine, so I got used to it and learned to block out the noise of his dissatisfaction. The Mona Lisa's smile returned for good use.

I could feel Zoe giving up on AJ. I don't blame her. There's only so much you can do for someone until they truly choose to help themselves. He is nowhere near ready, and part of me fears that he will never be. Have I lost him for all of eternity?

That night, when I returned, AJ was sitting on the bed in complete darkness. The look in his eyes was different, like it was not him. I slowly entered while keeping my eyes fixated on him. I put my bag down and proceeded to cautiously take a seat near him. I switched on the little lamp I had found the other day; the dimmer permitted me not to aggravate him with the brightness. I could tell he was high; the veins in his neck were fulminating, and his breathing was heavy. His hands were locked in fists, and both were placed on each knee. The person I was looking at was not my AJ; this was a stranger, and for the first time ever, I feared him.

I gently placed my hands on his, and I whispered his name. His hands loosened a little, but his breathing was still at a heavy pace. He began to cry, as I had never seen him cry before. Sobs of sorrow came from so deep within that he could barely breathe. I held him, and I let him empty his pain into me, and I absorbed as much of it as I could in hopes of removing some of his sorrow. I knew he was hurting, but I was hurting too, and I no longer had the strength to hurt for two. All I could do was hold him and hope that one day he would wake up.

"*I did this to you; I didn't protect you*," he sobbed as I held him. I knew he was still carrying the guilt from the mysterious night, and I still carried the anxiety of knowing the truth.

"*It's okay, it's ok*," I sang softly in his ear as I began to gently rock him. He laid his head on my lap, and his breaths began to slow down. I traced my fingers in his hair and around his now-tired facial features like I used to. His eyes began to slowly shut as I sang the song my mom used to sing to me when I would cry by the Carpenters.

"*Why do birds suddenly appear every time you are near? Just like me, they long to be close to you*."

After that night, I stopped hearing from Luna. I had messaged her almost every day for a week, but nothing. I would go sit at Crab Park at our usual time with a joint and my notebook. Still no sign of her. I began to worry about her. I hoped that her absence meant that she was in recovery or something. I remember her mentioning where her building was located, so after a week of not hearing from her, I decided I would make my way there and check in on her. I arrived at the destination I hoped to be, where she lived, so I rang the buzzer.

"*Yes?*" The voice in the box answered.

"*Hi, um, my name is Skye. I'm just looking for someone I am worried about; I believe she lives here.*" I explained with uncertainty.

"*And who is this person you speak of?*" The voice asked.

"*She goes by Luna? I am not sure if it's her real name,*" I replied. The voice went silent, and I heard the door unlock, so I pulled the door open and walked to the front desk. The young girl working motioned for me to take a seat.

I waited for about five minutes, and the young female eventually joined and sat next to me.

"*How do you know Luna?*" She began.

"*We met at Crab Park a while ago. We have writing sessions by the water at Crab Park,*" I shared.

"*Oh yes, you're Skye! I heard about you. Luna often spoke about you,*" she followed with sadness in her voice.

"*Spoke?*" I asked, feeling my heart drop.

"*Shit, yeah, sorry. Luna OD'd about a week ago. She found out some bad news about her family and was in rough shape from it. The last person to see her said she came to the using room to get some clean gear and then went back up to her room. The next day, she was found deceased during room checks,*" the female explained.

To my surprise, I instantly broke down into tears. I hated crying in front of strangers, but Luna had become my only true friend. She was so brilliant and beautiful. She did not belong in an empty room. She did not deserve to die in an empty room. Nobody does. Hearing this was devastating. Another frail young soul was failed by our corrupted society.

"*Illegitimi non carborundum...*" I whispered under my breath. The female heard, and we smiled, both in honour of Luna. She said that every time she parted ways with someone, they had better engrave that on her tombstone.

I slowly walked back with a heavy heart and a river of tears. So many tears had been shed by these eyes in such a short time that it was beginning to hurt physically. I made it home and found AJ smoking a joint in bed. I joined him and smoked in honour of my sweet friend Luna. I announced the news to AJ, to which he barely reacted. It almost felt as if he was relieved to get me back. He was never fond of the amount of time I spent with her. He didn't understand why this was so important to me, and I didn't expect him to.

We ended up getting into another argument that night—a big one too. Horrible and hurtful things were said, and AJ stormed off so angry, leaving me weeping in the room once again.

CHAPTER 12
THEY DO NOT SEE ME

I lay here brokenly, hoping and waiting for a chance to escape this horrid reality. It's been seven days since I last saw AJ. The last time I saw him he was on a bender, and our last words exchanged were quite malignant. He stormed off in the middle of it all and has not returned since. I have been a prisoner in this room for seven days, waiting, counting the seconds until he reappears. I've been smoking some of the harder stuff trying to block my thoughts. I can't help but think of all the worse scenarios. His recklessness has dawned heavily on him these days. His arcane disappearance remains an enigma I will never get over.

How did we let ourselves get sucked into this whirlpool of unfortunate, fucked-up events? I know we brought this upon ourselves, but sometimes I'd like to think that our shitty luck also played a big role.

I never asked for my mom to die, and I never asked for my dad to forget about me. I'm certain it was never a dream of mine as a little girl to end up in a shit hole like this and using drugs as an escape. They are all so desperate to get it from anyone just to feed this disease we call addiction. I am ashamed to admit the ludicrous things I've seen girls do to get their hands on drugs. Young and old, high like kites, too messed up to even realize what was going on, Old, perverted drug dealers were taking advantage of frail and desperate souls. I've never gotten to that point, not that it's not crossed my mind. There was a time I almost did, not for myself but for AJ. He was so dope-sick that it was making him unbearable, and he would become aggressive at times.

I want my AJ back—the real AJ. I feel so alone. I feel so angry. I feel betrayed by this world more and more every day. I roll a joint to try to calm my thoughts. I'm running low on my drugs, so I am trying to make it last until he returns. My hands are too shaky to roll. I've been trying for thirty minutes now, but I keep dropping the ground-up weed on the bed. I grab the dirty bong that's been used as an ashtray more than anything. I blow on it to get some of the dust off; I fill the bowl with weed, light it up, and let the smoke caress my lungs with its ashtray sweetness. I feel like writing. My mind is still racing. I pick up my marker and start scribbling down my thoughts on the wall. Getting lost in the vortex again.

I hate this world. These people I just cannot stand. It feels like no one will lend a hand unless it benefits them. We live in a world of narcissists, and I just can't stand it. I want to disappear. I don't want to be here. I cannot stand seeing the pain inflicted by another person's bitterness. We project, and we hurt people to make ourselves feel better, but at the end of the day, we all end up hurting from this. I hate this. I hate this world. I hate how it makes me feel. This seeping darkness comes crawling out every day, and I no longer have the strength to fight it away. Every time, it feeds off my misery and gets more powerful. It is overwhelming, and I feel myself fading. No one will understand, not even the people closest to me. They do not see me; they see the image they have mastered. They do not see beneath the surface. I am screaming for someone to hear me, but no one is paying attention. They don't pay attention to anything. They are convincing themselves that they are okay, but they are as blind as everyone else. Walking with no reason or meaning. Living life like it's just another day. Every day I ask myself if this is my last one. This time, I will be brave enough to cross over. Or will I be brave enough to walk away? It is when you are no longer here that they see your worth. It is when you disappear that they truly miss and acknowledge you. You can be here and yell as loud as your lungs will permit, and they will listen with a deaf ear and watch you suffer with blind eyes. I once heard that real eyes realize real lies. I have come to the understanding that those real eyes are so rare. Everyone has masked and filtered what they choose to see. Everyone lives in their own reality.

My eyes open, and it's already dark out. I must have fallen asleep while writing. Still no sign of AJ. I look around for any signs that he has been here while I was out cold, but everything looks the same. I could feel tears building up in my eyes. I can feel my heart slowly giving up. This loneliness is as present as it's ever been. Even more than when Mom passed. My stomach is howling for food. I can't recall when the last time was I ate. I make my way to the front office of the building to see what processed foods they have to offer us today. Nice, a dried, stale hot dog sauced with ketchup only, accompanied by 7 regular Lay's chips on the side. All the nutrients I need—I mean, not that I make much of an effort to eat healthily anyway. What's the point when I inject myself with garbage drugs? I eat the food; I can feel my body fighting back, but I have nothing else to offer it. I wash it down with a juice box. I tried to get a second one, but we are entitled to one juice box per day. It feels like I'm in a nut house, daycare, or zoo filled with junkies and fuckups, and I am now one of them. My crippling anxiety is slowly making its unwanted appearance as I can't stop thinking about AJ, and it is making me mental.

How could he leave me like this? We always said that no matter what, we were in this together, and now here I am, holding on to my last string of hope. He is all that I have left—all the reasons I still have the strength to wake up and make it through another day. But now he is gone, and I have become redundant to him.

I have no one else but him in my life, and I've now lost him too. There is no one to turn to for reassurance, for a hug, or for a shoulder to cry on. My pillow is the sole receiver of these everlasting tears, but it cannot hug me back no matter how tightly I squeeze. I walk the streets and feel eyes constantly judging me from every angle, probably thinking the worst of me. But what do they know? I've let myself go; I am aware, but I have nobody to look proper or beautiful for anymore. When I tried, he didn't even notice, so I stopped.

Society has shunned me, and my friends no longer want to hear my bullshit excuses. As for my dad, well, he's disappeared, most likely trying to gain as much distance from a fuckup like me as possible. I cannot blame them, as I hate myself too. This person, whom I see in the reflection of the mirror, is an intruder. This is not me. This is not who I wish to be; yet again, here I am, as fucked up as I can be. AJ, my love, has abandoned me with these torturing thoughts and questions my soul can never take again. I can no longer replay my mother's voice when she speaks, and I have not written to her in almost a year now. Everything in my mind has gone blurry, including her.

I look outside the window to see the sun glowing today, accompanied by a double rainbow. I have not left the room in the last 7 days, only to give my presence at the office. I figured maybe I should go out for a walk to absorb the sun and get some vitamin D in me, as I was most definitely in the negatives for that.

Double Rainbow on Hastings

Glowing Carnegie

Picture Credit: Rebekah BT

Edited By: Danielle Gillard

But first, a dreaded shower in the nasty bathroom. People would often shoot up and end up passing out and puking or shitting everywhere in there. But what other choice do I have? Beggars can't be choosers, as they say. I developed the habit of letting the hot water run for a couple of minutes before I stepped in, trying to eliminate as much bacteria as possible. After washing up, I quickly got dressed and headed out; that is when I bumped into this guy whom I had noticed frolicking in the building since we had moved here.

"*Sorry, love!*" He exclaimed after accidentally bumping into me.

"*That's all right!*" I replied with a faint smile and went on my unmerry way.

"*I'm Fabian, by the way!*" He shouted and returned a friendly smile.

"*Hi Fabian, I'm Skye*," I responded, pausing my steps to exit.

"*I've seen you around for a while now, but I never got the chance to introduce myself. I'm the maintenance guy! Not for this building because I live here, but for other buildings of this sort*," he shared while offering me a piece of chocolate.

"*Nice, now I know whom to come to if I need help with something*," I replied jokingly while biting into the chocolate.

"*Of course, I am a savant at many things. Plants, bikes, weed, whiskey, and more*," he confirmed with a laugh and confident grin.

"*Great, I can use help in all of that*," I disclosed, warming up to his kind manners.

"*Would you like to go smoke a joint? I have two rolled up, one each for safety*," he suggested.

"*Sure, why not? It's beautiful out*," I said, accepting his offer.

I was quite lonely and could use a joint in good company. We made our way out and walked over to Victory Square Park to sit in the grass. Fabian passed me one of the joints with a lighter; we cheered and proceeded to spark up. I already felt comfortable around him. He wasn't like the others in the building I had met so far. There was something different about him. We shared some things about ourselves while soaking up the sun and beautiful weather. Fabian had a lot to share. He was right about having a lot of knowledge about different things. He would go on for so long about subjects that it was hard to get a word in. But I made a game out of it in the end, as I humoured but also enjoyed his endeavours. He had shared that he no longer uses anything besides whiskey and marijuana, which here is like drinking Coca-Cola and eating candy. I was relieved to meet someone who didn't use drugs like the others. It was hard to connect with anyone. Everyone lives in their own imaginary world, and I refuse to let myself fall into that. I could not imagine seeing myself get worse. I've seen people stab or fight each other over the pettiest things. It's all about pride and respect here. But there is more pride than respect at times, so you can imagine the outcome.

Fabian and I spent most of the afternoon in the park chatting, and it helped me momentarily forget my agony and loneliness. It was one of the nicest days I had had in a while. To be frank, it was refreshing. Before parting ways, Fabian offered me a little bag of weed as a welcome gift and told me, if ever I needed more, to knock on door #506. I thanked him, we hugged, and we went on our separate ways to finish off the beautiful day.

As I made my way back to the Getti, I could feel my anxious mind take over, wondering if AJ had returned yet with the courage to tell me everything. With each step, I could feel my heartbeat getting louder throughout my entire body. I had forgotten my key, so Zach buzzed me in. I walked up the stairs, trying to calm my mind with positive affirmations I knew I did not truly believe in. But I was desperate for anything to help calm my nerves, as they had been in overdrive for quite some time now. Zoe had filed a missing person report after 72 hours of not seeing AJ, but still, nothing had turned up. As I passed by the office, I looked up at Zach, and he nodded *No,* knowing I was hoping AJ had come back. Every day a little piece of me died as I feared the worst for him, hoping he was safe despite being angry at his abandonment. I unlocked the door and paused before opening it, taking a deep breath alongside my wishful thinking that when I entered, he would be there waiting for me. I slowly opened the door, but he was not there. I stood there frozen for a while, trying to understand why the fuck I let myself get here. And for what? For whom? I have nobody and nothing left.

I pulled out the bag of weed that Fabian handed me and rolled a joint to help calm my thoughts. I smoked the whole thing; I wanted to completely shut down and forget, just for a little while. I did not want to feel anything, so I closed my blinds, shut my eyes, and off I went. I slept from 4 p.m. until 11 a.m. the next morning.

I woke up the next morning and decided I should step out to buy a good cup of coffee, as I could not stand to drink another shit-tasting coffee from the Getti. Coffee has always been a joy of mine, but that is now somewhat tainted by the cheap coffee served at our building. Most residents there like their coffee with half the cup filled with sugar and powdered creamer. I've heard that the creamer stuff could blow up if you lit it on fire, so I can only imagine the damage it is doing to our insides. Something else to add to the list of poisons we consume.

Today felt like a good day for a good cup of coffee. As I exited the building, I noticed an elderly gentleman with a walker, wearing a nice hat with a feather on it and a big leather jacket. I had seen him before in our building, but he mostly kept to himself and buried himself in his room. He was of a smaller figure, with a long, white, gray beard and gray hair to accompany it. His fingers were all bent up from arthritis and yellowed from the countless years of smoking. He had the sweetest smile I had seen in a while. Though his eyes were engraved with loneliness, they somehow complimented each other. I noticed him picking up weed and cigarette roaches from the ground one day, and I became curious about this individual, so I decided to approach him for a friendly conversation.

"*Hey, I'm Skye. I live in this building too*," I greeted them while offering him the joint roach in my pocket.

"*Hi! I've seen you. I'm Doug! I'm in room 507!*" He shared, happy to finish the last of it.

"*You're Fabian's neighbour, then*," I confirmed.

"*Pfff, that guy drives me nuts. He's always talking about this and that as if he knows everything*," Doug grunted while taking the joint with his arched, aching fingers.

"*Have you been neighbours for a long time?*" I questioned and was entertained by this old fellow's ways.

"*Yes, we have, and for way too long. I've lived in this block for over 12 years now*," he proudly exclaimed while pointing his index finger up in the air.

12 years... I could never, I thought to myself. But it seemed as if, for some people, it was all they knew.

"*Fabian thinks he runs the place because he does maintenance here sometimes, but he's not supposed to be. The rule is you can't work where you live*," he clarified with annoyance.

"*Oh, I see. He told me he works in other buildings as well*," I shared.

"*He says a lot of things*," Doug badgered while grunting other words I couldn't catch.

"*Things around here never go as they're supposed to. More than half the people here are idiots*," he continued.

I figured it was best I changed the subject to not stir up the poor old guy too much.

"*What are you doing out here? Are you waiting for someone*?" I asked, curious about what he was up to standing here alone.

"*No, I am panhandling. I go down by the Port to the same location almost every day, but some stupid lady is there singing today. She's not even good, and she knows that's my spot! There's always a bunch of people from the cruise boats that wander there, so it's the best place to make a good buck*," he fumed while banging on his walker.

"*I even made a new sign today. Look!*" He exclaimed while proudly showing off his sign. It read:

ACCEPTING DONATIONS TO HELP SAVE THE SOUTH POLE FREE RANGE CHICKENS.

"*Clever! If I had some spare change, I'd give it to you after reading that.*" I laughed.

I felt kind of bad for the fellow. I took an instant liking to him; he was grumpy about everything, but in a way that brought a sort of joy to me.

"*What are you up to?*" He returned the question, looking up at me with his tired little eyes.

"*I'm on* my way to *get a good coffee; I don't like the coffee here*," I stated with a squint.

"*I hear you." I only drink it because it is free*," he replied with a slight chuckle.

"*Would you like to join me for a coffee? I'll buy*," I offered, longing for the company as well.

"*Sure, if it's from Tim Hortons, I'm in!*" He happily accepted.

"*I can't afford anywhere else*," I said, laughing at the truth of it.

"*Nowadays, a coffee shop sells a cup for $8 a pop and expects a tip on top of it. What is this world we reside in?"* I followed. Doug agreed and, again, confirmed that we live in a world filled with idiots.

We made our way to the nearest Tim Hortons very slowly, as he was moving with an old, busted-up walker filled with trinkets and lights. We finally arrived at our destination; I ordered a large coffee with one milk, and he ordered one large coffee with six sugars and four creams. We grabbed our cups and found a bench to sit on while we enjoyed our *Timmie's* coffee. We sat in silence for a while, savouring the warmth and flavour of the delightful liquid.

"*Do you have any pets?*" he asked, breaking the silence.

"*Nope, do you?*" I inquired myself.

"*Yep, I have one rat. His name is Spirit! You can meet him when we go back home*," he rejoiced.

"*I've never had a pet rat, but I have heard they are great companions,*" I noted.

"*I've had 41 rats in my life, and they are the best partners. I also have a pet spider named Lilly*," he shared.

"*41 pet rats! And a pet spider! Like a tarantula?*" I quavered, shocked at everything I was hearing.

"*Also, Lilly is a beautiful name. It's my best friend's nam*e," I added, feeling sad about her lack of presence in my life.

"*No, just a regular little spider. She has lived in the corner of my kitchen counter for almost a year now*," he explained, smiling from ear to ear.

"*I leave her be, and she eats the other bugs that come crawling in. I think she might be pregnant right now because she looks fatter than usual*," he jeered, followed by a wheezing laugh.

"*Aren't you afraid she's going to lay eggs everywhere in your place?*" I replied, a little unsettled by the news.

"*Also, never call a female fat if you don't want to suffer the consequences*," I teased.

"*Well, it is what it is. It's her home, too*," He affirmed.

"*And trust me, I've learned that the hard way. But Lilly is not your typical woman*," he replied, laughing so hard he almost lost his breath.

This was a first. I had never heard of somebody having a pet spider like that and having the utmost empathy and respect for it. Nor have I ever heard of anyone having 41 pet rats, either, but Doug was built differently. He found a way to love the unwanted, maybe because that's how he felt himself. His eyes spoke for him. I did not have to ask him to know the pain of his loneliness, as I knew it all too well myself. I enjoyed his company; he often made me laugh with his cantankerous speeches about this crazy world, and he brought a dark yet innocent humour to our pain.

He also did not use drugs. He mentioned that he occasionally drank and smoked weed if he could find some. He had no shame in sharing his adventures in searching for leftover weed roaches on the sidewalks. He claims he's found over 100 roaches in one day. He also goes dumpster diving behind the weed shops when they get rid of their old stuff. Quite the resilient and clever old man, I must say, as I would have never thought of that.

"*Maybe one day you can take me on one of your dumpster dive missio*ns," I urged, as I would benefit from some free dumpster weed from time to time.

"*Sure, but you get 30%, and I get the rest.*" He agreed and was generous enough to share some of his findings with me.

We shook on it as per Doug's request, making it more official. The night was setting in, and my frail new friend was getting cold, so we agreed to make our way back to the building. Once we arrived, I dreaded returning to an empty room, so I said my goodbyes to Doug and was on my way to walk around, attempting to escape my bitter thoughts. Doug called out my name and waved for me to walk back over to him. As I got closer, I noticed him looking at me differently.

"*Are you all right, little bird? I sense the sadness in you. I did not want to mention it earlier as we are new friends, but as I watched you walk away, I could not help but notice it more,*" he shared with his sweet old eyes searching for an answer.

"*I'm all right, Dougy; I'm just thinking about stuff, you know*," I explained, looking down at my feet.

"*Well, I know just the thing to cheer you up whenever you feel dow*n," he said with a smile hidden by his white mustache and beard. I chuckled and waited for him to continue.

He began to sing a song with his tired vocal cords and deepened voice. I was shocked when I began to recognize the melody; it was the song my mother used to sing to me, *Close to You* by the Carpenters. My eyes began to fill with tears. I grabbed hold of both of Doug's hands as he continued to sing to me, joyful at my reaction. When he finished, I could not help but hug the old man, and I thanked him. Through Dougy, my mother spoke to me. She came to me to soothe me with our song. Doug held a special place in my heart. Though he was angry at the world, and so was I, we found a way to beautifully be angry together.

I went on my way, a smile still on my face and my cheeks glistering from the wetness of the left-over tears.

These last 24 hours have been the best I've had in a while. God, the universe, life, or whatever it was, had blessed me with two kind souls that made me feel a little less alone.

I made a third friend that night once my serotonin high from the day went away. I found a baggie behind the bed that carried some unknown drug. It was either up or down. Nevertheless, I craved it, so I did it. I missed AJ, but I did not want to because it hurt too much. I continued to use it every second or third day until the pain became unbearable. All I had to do was walk down Hastings Street and wait for someone to walk by me, offering whatever they had on them. Sometimes, I would get it for free by being "beautiful," as they would blindly claim. I knew I was not being safe; it was like playing Russian Roulette with drugs. Some of the dope I would get was so bad I would be benzo'd and out for full days. Meanwhile, my back began to ache more and more as I would pass out in the most uncomfortable ways for hours on end.

On sober days, I would often hang with Dougy in the afternoon. He would serenade me with his songs and stories while we sipped coffee. We would sometimes take his rat,

Spirit, for walks when the sun was out. In the evenings, I would drink beers or whiskey and share joints with Fabian after his working day. I was grateful that life graced me with them; they were the only good things I had to look forward to these days. I kept my distance from Zoe, as I knew she saw right through me, but I could not admit it to her. I refused to.

It's been 3 weeks now, and there's still no sign of AJ. At this point, there can only be two outcomes: AJ left me here to rot alone, or he is dead somewhere rotting alone. Whatever it was, it was me, myself, and I from now on.

Dougy with Burger

Dougy with Sign

Picture Credit: Rebekah BT

Edited By: Danielle Gillard

CHAPTER 13
THE PAYPHONE

One morning, I found the courage to walk over to the payphone and make a phone call I had been avoiding for a while now. But at this point, I had nothing left to lose. My fingers were trembling as I dialed the numbers, dreading the next one until I punched in the last one. At least I still remembered my father's phone number.

Ring, ring, ring, ring... No answer. I hang up before the answering machine eats my quarters.

I try one more time: ring, ring, ring, ring... Same thing, no answer.

This time I attempted to leave a message, but once I heard the beep, I froze for five seconds, and then I hung up.

I stood there for about 2 minutes, trying to regain access to the courage I had built up. I picked up the phone and dialed another number, feeling just as nervous as the first call. My conversation with Doug had me thinking about Lilly. I missed her a lot. She was the only stable friend I had; she knew how to ground me, and I had pushed her away.

Ring, ring, ring...

"*Hello?*" I heard her voice on the other line. I froze again.

"*Hello!?*" She repeated.

"*Lilly?*" I trembled to hold my emotions back.

"*Yes?*" She replied, not recognizing me.

"*It's Skye*," I whispered to her, feeling that I didn't deserve this phone call.

"*Skye! Oh. My. Shit. Where have you been?*" Lilly cried out of joy and relief.

"*I've been looking for you and trying to find a way to contact you for months. I thought you were dead!*" She followed, breaking down in tears. I joined her for a while, and then, finally, the sobbing fest ended.

"*I'm so sorry. It's been so fucked, Lilly. I was too embarrassed to face you guys. But I can't do this anymore, Lils. I can't. I...*" choked up by my loss of breath, I could not control my emotions.

"*Where are you living now?*" Lilly inquired with a soft and loving tone.

"*I'm still at the same place in the Downtown Eastside*," I told her, already picturing her facial expressions.

"*Like in an apartment or...?*" She followed.

"*Not really. I mean, we have our room, but in one of those SRO buildings I told you about*," I continued, feeling my grip tighten as a result of the shame.

"*Oh, shit, okay. Wow, um. Are you okay? I mean, obviously, you've been better. Do you need anything? What can I do? How can I help?*" Lilly bombarded me with questions, anxious to be of help.

"*I'm all right, Lils. I'm looking for AJ. I'm worried about him. I haven't seen him in a week. He hasn't been doing well at all*," I shared, sharing a feeling of relief from confiding in someone I truly trusted.

"*Have you called the police?*" She wondered if it would be the normal thing to do. But not here.

"*There is no point. We're just junkies from the DTES. But the workers from my building put in a missing person report,*" I explained.

"*Shit, well, I hope he turns up alive soon. But, um, Skye, there are some things I do have to tell you. I know it's probably just going to add to everything, but there isn't a right time to tell you this*," Lilly quivered, and I could hear her take a deep breath. I waited in silence, afraid of what I was about to hear.

"*Your dad died three months ago from liver cancer. He waited too long before being seen by the doctor; the cancer spread due to his negligence, and he passed away. I've been looking for you everywhere so I could tell you,*" she followed.

We stayed in silence for what seemed to be a couple of minutes, but really, I was unsure of how long it had been. A wave of emotions filled my heart, and part of me was not grasping the reality of it. My life has felt like a nightmare these days, but this was the cherry on top of it all. My father was no longer sitting in his recliner, drinking, smoking, or sleeping. Now, even if I did want to go back, I no longer had my home. I grew up in that house. My mother's memories live there alongside the miserable ones I try to forget.

"*Skye, are you still there?*" Lilly asked, breaking the silence.

"*Yes, Lils, sorry, I'm just...*" I tried to explain, but I could not find the words.

"*I get it. I mean, I don't. But I get what you are trying to say. There are no words to say to make this go away or feel okay, really.*" She followed, always knowing the best thing to say to me.

"*There's another thing, unfortunately. Em is not doing too well, either. She is in psychiatric care right now. She was at a party this summer; she had taken some drugs this random guy gave her, and she went into a major psychosis. They had to call the police and ambulance because she ended up out in the street half naked and confused. She had no idea where or who she was. I've gone to visit her a couple of times, but she's still not fully recovered. The doctors say it was triggered by the drugs and her genetics.*"

"*What, are you serious?! I need to go see her!*" I responded in total shock.

"*I don't think that's a good idea, Skye. No offence, but you don't seem to be in a good position yourself, and I am afraid it might only do more damage to the both of you,*" Lilly replied.

I stayed silent, annoyed at the truth of it all.

"*I miss you, Skye. I'd love to see you grab a coffee or lunch.*" She proposed.

The thought of letting Lilly see me in this state brought on a wave of anxiety. There was no way I could face her like this. I could not let that happen, no matter what.

"*Soon, Lilly, I promise. I need to get better and do better first,*" I explained, sad to feel like I was hurting my caring friend once again.

"*But I can help you, Skye. I want to be there for you,*" Lilly replied, begging for a chance.

At that moment, I felt my heart break as I knew I had to push her away for her own good. Lilly was too delicate for someone like me. She was a tulip, and I was a rose; my thorns would pierce through her little heart. I understood that I had to love her from a distance to protect her from me. Lilly would give her all for the people she loved, and I could not taint her with my darkness. Silly me, no one can keep such a beautiful, delicate flower for themselves. I knew the only way I could do this was by making her an empty promise, and so I did, feeling each word break my heart a little more. I told her I would call her this Friday to make plans, knowing that I would not. When I said goodbye to Lilly, I made sure to let her know my appreciation for her. Therefore, she cannot carry guilt for my selfish mistakes. When we hung up, I prayed to hear her voice again someday when the sun shined brighter in my direction.

I stood in the phone booth for a while without moving. My mind was trying to assess everything that had just filtered through. My dad was gone, and so was Em, in a way. I had to stay away from Lilly for her sake, and AJ had been gone for days. I had nobody left to lose but myself at this point, and it's not like I was all that and a bag of chips anyway.

I kept replaying my last moment with my father when I gave him that last hug. Part of me now wishes I had stayed, even though it would have tortured him to let me see him that way. I never thought I would feel this way, but I would do anything to go back to my father's place now. I can't believe that he is gone—not that he was ever there for me, but physically. He's gone.

As I stood there with my thoughts, Alex's face popped into my mind. Maybe my soul was desperate to feel safe. All I wanted was to curl up in a ball in his arms and hear his reassuring and loving words fill my ears. I felt the instinct to pick up the phone again and dial his number, one of the few numbers I remembered by heart.

Ring, ring, ring, ring, ring...

"*Hi, you've reached Alex. I can't come to the phone right now, but you know what to do if you want me to call you back. Or you can just text me because it's 2023.*"

I had not heard his voice in so long. I instantly broke down. I spent all my change calling his number and listening to his voice, grasping at whatever I could to make my heart feel better. After the fourth and last time, he picked up.

"*Yes?*" I heard the voice say something on the other end of the line.

"*Hello? Who is this?*" He followed due to my silence.

"*Alex...*" I whispered with a smile.

"*Yeah, this is he!*" He replied, seeming confused by this call, understandably.

I remained silent. My heart was pounding in my chest as all I wanted to do was cry to him, but I knew it wouldn't be fair after all this time.

"*Skye?*" I suddenly heard him say it, and I broke down.

I sobbed and sobbed and sobbed, and he stayed on the line with me and waited until I was done.

"*Skye, where are you?*" He inquired.

"*At a phone booth*," I replied, embarrassed to share my location.

"*Okay, which phone booth? What street?*" He persisted.

"*Why are you asking?*" I whispered, already knowing the answer.

"*I'm coming to pick you up, Skye*," he said firmly, sounding worried.

"*I can't let you do that, Alex*," I responded, feeling my heart oppose my words.

"*Why not? Lilly and I have been worried sick about you. I'm not here to lecture or judge you. I just want you to be safe*," he followed, trying to convince me.

"*You don't understand*," I heaved, only wishing he could.

"*Then let me! Let me understand and help you. Stop being stubborn for once in your life, Skye. Please!*" He pleaded with a crack in his voice.

"*But don't you get it, Alex? I am no good for anyone, not even myself. I have hurt you with my fucked-up ways enough times. You don't, and you never did deserve it. I never deserved you*," I fretted.

"*Skye, that doesn't matter, and it's okay. I know you, and I know who you really are. This isn't you. You are just lost. You can get better, and we are here for you. We are your family*." He sniffled, not knowing what else to say. He knew that arguments with me were always a losing game, and that had not changed.

"*Alex, I know you don't understand, and that is okay. I need to stay away from you and Lilly; I am toxic, and my conscious will no longer let me hurt anyone with my selfish ways. Just please promise me one thing*," I wept while gripping both my hands to the phone so tightly I could feel the blood escaping my fingertips.

"*Okay,*" he replied with sadness and defeat in his voice.

"*Please remember me for me. Remember all that we used to be. Stay away from me until I am free from this addiction. And when you do think of me, please do not feel pity or sorrow. I ask that you only keep the good memories of me,*" I fretted, with tears rolling down my face.

"*Skye, why are you talking like that?*" He asked with doubt.

"*Because you never know what the next day will be,*" I replied softly, finding peace in this truth.

"*I love and will always love you, Alex,*" I said, knowing this was my cue.

"*Sky-*"

Click. I hung up. It hurt so fucking much, but I knew I did the right thing for both. I made my way back to the Getti and found myself fixated on finding a hit. I had not touched it in a while, but I needed to numb myself before I did something worse. This pain and guilt I just could not take anymore; my cup was overflowing, and I needed to make it stop.

CHAPTER 14
SCALING THE DEPTHS

As I entered the building, I put my hoodie on to hide my face. I was not in the mood to speak with anyone unless they had some drugs to give me. Other than that, everyone could just fuck off. I had nothing left to lose; I had already lost every single person I loved, and it was not like I was worth much at this point. Just another waste of breath, tainting everything she touches. I despised myself, and I gave up the only true friends I ever had for someone who would leave me here to rot alone. Maybe this is what I deserved. I mean, things happen for you and not to you, right?

I went up to my room and stood in front of my door, waiting until I spotted Spaz. He was the only one in the building I trusted to front me of drugs since I had no money. After about 20 minutes, I heard his high-pitched nasal voice coming from the stairs, and my heart instantly began to pound. I knew I was being stupid, but I did not care. I just wanted to be numb and feel nothing. As he made his arrival on the second floor, he noticed me and, as usual, complimented me. I would always thank him without making further conversation, but today was a different day.

I signaled for him to come closer, and he looked around, unconvinced that I was looking at him. I confirmed with a nod that I was signaling for him to make his way to me. We entered my room, and I sat on my bed, battling my inner demons in my mind. After a couple of minutes of silence, he began to seem uneasy and finally broke the silence.

"*What can I do for you, darling?*" He questioned me, looking around, paranoid as if I was setting him up.

"*I need a fix. You said to come to you if ever I needed anything when I first moved here*." I shuddered to regret my words instantly.

"*Uh, okay. Are you sure you're not just in your feelings, baby girl? You've never asked me once for a fix since you've lived here. I would hate to be the cause of destruction to such a beautiful creation, and you seem pretty upset right now*." He hesitated while observing me in a worried manner.

"*No, no. Trust me, it's only for tonight. I just had a fucked-up day, and I need to numb myself before I do something stupid. And don't worry. The destruction has already started long ago. Your hands are clean*," I followed with my shaking voice.

"*Okay, okay. Well, for my and your safety, may I stay with you while you do your hit to supervise you? And if I see you're all good, I'll leave you be. I've already got too many deaths on my drug dealing belt, and I would hate to add you to the list*," he insisted with a humbleness that I would be stupid to refuse.

"*Yeah, that's fine.* Also, I have no money right now, I'll get you back when I do, *and don't try anything stupid. I have ways to know*" I warned, hoping to induce a little bit of fear in him still. I did not have any way of knowing.

He pulled a stash out of his bag and placed it on the table. He verified for a second time if I truly wanted to go through with this, and this time I answered *Yes* with no hesitation.

I asked Spaz if he could prep it for me and shoot me up as if it would remove some of the guilt from what I was about to do.

I put some music on and watched him prepare my hit with such delicacy that I almost felt honoured until I reminded myself what he was about to inject into my veins. Once he finished, he enlaced my left arm with the blue tie wrap, waited for my veins to make their appearance, and slowly inserted the venom into the chosen one. Within the first fifteen seconds, I could feel my head weigh heavily and my eyelids shut. He then laid me on my bed and sparked a joint for himself while taking a seat on the chair across from me. I knew he was there; I felt his presence, but I could not acknowledge him. I was in my own world and too high to speak. He eventually left, though I could not tell you how much time had passed. I fell asleep shortly after, which was probably for the best.

I woke up to find a baggie with drugs and a can of Sprite by my bedside. Next to it was a note from Spaz saying,

"*Yo. I hope you enjoyed the ride. I hope the pain escapes for a while. Here's a little extra, and a can of Sprite. C'ya around, kid. Spaz*,"

Though I knew he was no good for me to have around, I had an appreciation for his thoughtful ways. I opened the can of Sprite and chugged it because I was so dehydrated. I had no idea how long I had been asleep, but it was now 2 p.m. the next day. My right arm was numb from falling asleep on it, and it took a while to regain full access to my flexibility and strength.

I made my way down to the office to announce my presence and foolishly hoped to hear any news about AJ. Zach was in today, and he looked in rough shape, probably from a hangover, I would guess. As I expected, there was no news from AJ, and he was indeed hungover. I heard Zoe's office door open, and a faint voice called out my name. I poked my head out to assess the situation and saw Zoe waving for me to step into her office. She shut the door behind us and offered me a sandwich. I gracefully accepted; turkey sandwiches were my favourite.

"*How are you holding up, Skye? Still, no sign of AJ, I hear*," she stated with sadness in her eyes.

"*I've been better. I just want AJ to come back. At this point, I am starting to wonder if he is still alive. It's so unlike him*," I responded, feeling a crack in my voice.

"*Well, I've been phoning the police every day to try and push it, but you know how it is down here*," she replied.

"*I wish they would take this more seriously*," I breathed while taking my first bite.

"*I know, Skye. Me too. I see this happen all the time, and I feel so helpless*," she replied while preparing some tea.

"*I've been seeing so many signs of people missing. What's going on with that?*" I asked, hating that I was about to add AJ to that list.

"*Honestly, it's getting scary. I read that last year there were approximately 5,500 missing person reports in Vancouver, which is now an all-time high. I fear walking alone in the evenings sometimes when I finish my shift*," she admitted.

"*That's crazy and creepy. Humanity has completely lost it. I'm going to walk around today with his picture in the hope that he has been seen somewhere*," I said, understanding that I was on my own for this.

"*Just be safe, Skye. You have my number if you need anything*," she insisted.

I made my way back into my room, showered, changed my clothing, found the most recent picture of AJ, and made my way to the streets. I walked down to Crab Park at first since AJ loved sitting by the water and drinking at that spot. I figured maybe he had made a friend and was on a bender, and as much as it angered me to think he would do that, I still hoped that I would find him there. I began to walk by the tents, asking people who were hanging around. They all gave the same answer I feared, except for one guy who "*thinks he remembers*" seeing him around a couple of days ago, but I think he was just trying to be the hero and tease me with false hope. Once I scoured through the park, I began to walk back towards Hastings Street.

I was not feeling the greatest from getting high last night, but I knew I could not bear to sit in my room and wait for something to happen or for someone to care enough to help. If AJ was in trouble, it was up to me to find him and help him. I started by visiting the homeless shelters. Even though I knew how much he despised going there, I had nothing to lose. None of the shelters knew of him, so I wandered the streets for the entire day, asking every passerby and receiving the same horrid answer over and over again. *Where are you, AJ?* An unsettling feeling that something was not right was taking over.

During my search, I wandered into a back alley that seemed busy with people from the community. I began to ask around and noticed most of the people there were walking up to this door and giving their names. I asked a woman next to me what this place was, and she informed me that this was a Safe Injection Site. I had heard about these places before but had yet to see one. The girl could see my curiosity and asked if I was interested in trying it out. I was still unsure of how this all worked, so she walked me to the door and knocked, and a young man about my age opened. The girl explained that I was new to this, so he invited me to come in for a quick tour and explanation.

I stepped in and saw what was waiting for me inside.

"*Before getting a table assigned, you must inform the person working at the door which drugs you are using today. We mark it down, along with your handle, your table number, and the time you got your table assigned. This helps us keep track of drug use and overdose histories. There are ten tables, each of them numbered. The ones that are in use have an orange cone on them, accompanied by the same number.*

Once you are done using your table, please return your cone to the front desk. The limited time for table use is 30 minutes. If you get Benzo'd, we add an extra 30 minutes in hopes that you wake up. Once the hour is up, if you are still unconscious, we will bag your belongings and put your name on them. This does not mean we are responsible for any lost items. To prevent this from happening, we suggest that once you are done prepping your fix, you put away your belongings and then shoot up. Many people forget this and wake up with their belongings missing, and it has started many physical altercations here," he explained so quickly I could barely keep up.

"*If that is the case, we place you in the resting corner where all the benzo'd people go. We keep an eye on them until they are feeling better.*" He followed, pointing to the corner where there were two people on mattresses, completely out of it.

"*Any questions before I proceed?*" He asked. I nodded, still focused on the two fellow users.

"*If you are disrespectful towards the staff or the other clients in any way, you will get a temporary or permanent ban, depending on the gravity of the situation,*" he continued.

"*What's your name and your handle?*" He proceeded to ask.

"*My name is Skye, and I don't have a handle*," I informed him while looking around.

"*Well then, let's find you one, shall we? Any ideas?*" He questioned.

"*Not really. Can't I just use my real name?*" I replied, dreading having to do this. If I gave myself a handle, then it would make me an official "*crackhead*".

"*Sure, if that's what you prefer*," he shrugged.

"*Or, I guess Skye Baby is fine. That's what my boyfriend calls me*," I shared, feeling my heart break a little as I said those words.

"*Okay, cool, so your name is Skye, and your handle is Skye Baby. So, are you looking to use a table today? We have some available right now if you are*," he shared, pointing to the tables.

"*Sure, I'll try it out*," I mumbled, still feeling a little unsure.

At the end of the day, it's better than me shooting up alone in my room, right?

Handle: Skye Baby

Drug: Down and Side

Table: 4

Time of Arrival: 4:36 PM

Time of Exit: ________

I sat down at my table and looked around to observe what the others were doing. I felt like such an intruder. I knew I didn't belong there. I took out my supplies and placed them on the table, and I picked up the bundle of harm-reduction gear that was waiting for me as I took my seat. I unwrapped the blue tie that was holding the bundle together and separated the tools while placing them in order. I looked to my right at the woman sitting next to me, as I could feel her inspect my every move. I smiled, and she smiled back and offered me some gummies.

"*My name is Bootsy; I chose that because I have a boot obsession*," she stated while letting out a loud, obnoxious laugh.

"*Nice, I'm Skye. Thanks for the gummies*," I replied, trying to have a short conversation without being rude about it.

"*You're new here. I've never seen you before*," she noticed.

"*Yep, my first time here*," I confirmed with an annoyed smile.

The woman was so high that she was moving in all directions and could not keep still. Her arms were flaring all over the place as she paraded around her table. One of the staff finally got upset and demanded that she remain in her seat, to which she replied with a loud *Fuck Off, Goof.* She then continued lollygagging and yelling profanities at the people around her.

The staff packed her belongings and escorted her out, giving her a one-week bar, which she was not delighted about. I could hear her yelling more insults from the back alley for the next five minutes until she finally gave up and wobbled away, yelling at her new victim.

I was able to finally focus on my fix again now that she was gone. As I was about to begin the process, I suddenly heard someone yell out, *"I need a doctor. Can anyone doctor me?"*

The individual next to me stood up and proposed to help him, which brought me total confusion as he did not seem to be fit to be a doctor. I observed what happened next and was shocked by it all. The man requesting the doctor lay on the floor and turned his head to the side. The helper then took the needle and injected him in the neck. One of the staff members noticed my uncertainty and came to my rescue with an explanation.

"Don't worry. I reacted the same way on my first day. I was frantically searching for an actual doctor until I explained what it meant. When someone can no longer shoot up in their usual spots due to excessive scabbing and

bruising, they eventually begin shooting up in their necks. If they aren't comfortable doing it themselves with the mirrors we offer, they yell out for a doctor, and a fellow client who is willing will help them will assist. So, this is basically what you have just witnessed here," he explained while we both kept our eyes locked on the situation.

"*I feel like I am learning so much in one day*," I joked, feeling uneasy about it all.

I returned my concentration to my fix, but I could not complete the process. The worker I had just spoken to noticed me struggling and offered to help me out.

"*You won't get in trouble for doing that?*" I was a little confused by this place.

"*Nope, I do it often, as sometimes some people have the shakes. We can only prepare it for you, though. You must inject yourself, we aren't aloud to do it for you. You can also ask a fellow client at a table to do it for you if you are comfortable with that*," he explained while prepping my fix.

Once he was done, he wrapped the tie around my arm and handed over the needle that was now filled with venom. I thanked him and waited for him to give me a little bit of privacy, not that there was much here anyway. I took a deep breath and inserted the needle into my most prominent vein. I slowly pushed the syringe down, and I could feel the liquid creeping its way through my vein. I sat in my chair, staring at the wall, waiting for the numbness to resurface and take over. My eyes shut for what seemed to be a little while until someone tapped on my table to wake me up.

"*It's been almost an hour, love. You've got to get moving and leave room for the people waiting outside*," the young man declared.

I took 5 minutes to regain my senses, packed my belongings, returned the orange cone, and stepped out. After that day, I returned there on many occasions to get high since I felt safer there than alone in my room, though I did miss writing on my walls. Tired from the long day, I walked back to the Getti, counting every excruciating step.

On my way back, three sketchy-looking guys walked past me, and one of them let out a low "*stupid bitch"* under his breath. Their faces seemed familiar, but I could not remember how I knew them. I continued to walk without reacting to the insult to avoid confrontation. For the rest of the night, I could not get their faces out of my head, trying to recall where I had seen them before. I lay in bed and smoked a joint to try and calm my thoughts. *Shit, it must have been a Sativa because I can feel the vortex taking over*. I picked up the marker and began to write until my wrist hurt too much to continue.

When you realize your ideas of your own identities are not fully formed, merely faintly developed buds that first expose themselves to the perils of public life.

It's not okay to give yourself to one person and allow them to have unwarranted, unrequested control over the way you look at things and the decisions you make about your own life.

It's not fair to either of you, really.

In the stillness of the summer night, we lay awake under that tree, and we held onto our dreams.

We held on to what we wanted from each other.

We held on to a warm body—a warm, loving, and welcoming body.

A safety blanket in an uncertain, cold, and grating world.

We had a unified dream. We dreamed of our seed, the one we planted in each other that day.

We barely knew each other, and we already saw our future together.

It was beautiful, and I still longed for that night under those stars.

That everlasting pretense of intense affection and dedication, emotion, and now an obsession.

But don't you see? It's all just a beautiful betrayal. Just another fleeting, self-defeating memory. Just another chance at simplicity, gone because complexity is the driving force of creativity and of beating naivety.
Remember the night I told you never to turn your back on me, and I told you I would not turn my back on you?
I said, My love, don't you do it to me because we were too good to just forget.
But to my chagrin, you did forget.
You're still in my heart, and I miss you so much, but maybe it's for the best.
I do love you; don't you see how much it kills me to let you go?
But my life is taking a back seat to our love, and it keeps me up at night.
I'm sick of it. I'm sick of being alone. I'm sick of getting high. I'm sick of the petty games and the selfish, childish ways you choose.
I'm sick of trying to understand why you left me here to rot.
I need someone to accept my endlessly flawed personality. I need someone I can accept.
I need not be changed to fit another's image of myself.
I am my own, different, I know, and your narrow-minded vision does not include me or my world.

I am complicated and flawed but still beautiful like everyone else.
We are all beautiful in our own ways, even with the ugliness of pain.
There may be comfort in simplicity, but it is not for me, and it won't ever be.
There are more layers to me that I don't want to be peeled off for my true self to be revealed.
I would feel a bit too exposed and not as composed as I'd like to be, and despite this, I still wanted to reveal myself to you in time.
My love, my sweet immersion, I must let you go, but I know deep down I cannot.
I have waited and waited in hopes of seeing you again, and I will always wait.
Even though it's been months now, and you have yet to come back for me.
Even though you might not come back for me. Even though you might never come back for me.
I will wait for you. You will rue the day you ever left my side.

I have now become a nyctophile. The night refused to let me sleep with the screams and cries from the streets. A broken symphony imposing itself on my ears that I no longer wished to hear, but there was nothing I could do besides lay here in fear. I feared that one of those cries was yours, and I would not even know because they all sounded the same. Lost souls wandering the streets, gambling with death as they search for a way to escape.

Wanderers of the Alley

Picture Credit: Danielle Gillard

CHAPTER 15

WAR IN THE STREETS

I woke up at 4 a.m. drenched in sweat once again, but perhaps with some answers to my burning questions. I had this nightmare that felt like a replay of the night I do not remember. Everything felt so real. The events matched the physical evidence from our cuts and bruises. Though I did not want to believe this to be the truth, deep down, I knew it was. I now remembered how I recognized the lads from yesterday.

In my nightmare, I could see myself as if I were floating and watching from above.

I was with AJ, and we were hanging out with three guys and one girl. We were in a room that looked a little like ours but was in a different small building. We smoked some crack that was offered to us by the fellow from yesterday. AJ and I got knocked out by the hit, but somehow the others did not, though they claimed to have also smoked. One of the lads checks on AJ, who was passed out in a chair, to verify his state and see if he is truly out of it. He was. The lad nodded yes to the others, who then began to form a circle around me on the bed, including the female, who was high out of her mind. She poked me, first on my arm, then my side; she proceeded to move to my cheeks and then poked my breast, but I did not wake up. She began to lift my shirt up to my neck and then stopped. She looked up at the guys, waiting for someone to go next. One by one, they began to slowly undress me while chuckling together and laughing at AJ's inability to protect me. My pants, shirt, and bra were now removed, and I was left with my underwear and my dirty socks. Hands were groping me in places they should not be touching.

AJ slowly began to gain consciousness and notice what was happening, but at first, he was too weak from his hit to react instantly. Eventually, the heaviness wore off, and AJ launched himself at the abusers, but he could not hold his ground. They began to beat him up, and the chaos woke me up. I tried to help AJ, but I could not move as the girl was holding me back. After a few seconds, I found all the strength I had left and elbowed the girl in the nose, waiting for her to release me. She regained her grip on me quickly and fought back in a fury from the blow. Her last punch was what woke me from my nightmare, and here I am now, left with a new set of questions and fears.

I broke down in tears, feeling hopeless and helpless at the same time. I wondered if AJ had left me due to the pain and guilt he was carrying from that night. He kept saying things like *I did not protect you* or *I did this to you.* Is this why he left me? Where would he go? He had no money, no phone, and nobody to turn to that I knew of. I began to play the worst scenarios in my head and continued to cry until my body refused to serve me more tears.

I jumped out of bed and made my way back out to Hastings, determined to find him once and for all. I marched my weak body to the street to find myself standing in front of complete anarchy. The city had initiated a street sweep to clear Hastings Street, but this time it was done with much more force than it had ever been done before. The police had blocked off intersections and shut down the street. I could see torn-up tents in the middle of the street alongside people's belongings. The police were throwing away their belongings and homes with such dehumanization that it made me feel sick. People were protesting and fighting back in the streets, trying to protect their freedom. I could hear a woman yelling at the police from afar, saying, "*We are only trying to survive here; we have nothing left. You will displace us until we all end up dying!*" Tears began to flow again; I was surprised I had any left to give. I can no longer bear to witness this violence, pain, and discrimination. Why must it be this way?

In the streets of our city, a war rages on,

Between those with power and those who have none.

Police armed with force and the homeless with their plight,

The battle lines are drawn in a never-ending fight.

The streets are the stage, and the violence is the play,

Where the homeless and addicts are hunted day after day.

Their lives are mere commodities, just a game,

In the war of the streets, they're caught in the flame.

The police come with guns, and the homeless with despair,

Each side with a weapon, each side with a prayer.

The sound of gunfire echoes through the night,

As the battle for the streets rages on with might.

The homeless cry out for help; their voice is ignored,

Their homes are on the streets, and their safety is deplored.

They long for a life free from fear and pain,

But in the war of the streets, their cries are in vain.

The police fight for order, safety, and the law,

While the homeless suffer from deep and raw wounds.

The war in the streets is a profound tragedy,

As both sides suffer with no common ground.

But amidst the chaos, a little hope still remains,

As hearts join together to break the chains.

Of the war in the streets, Police Versus Homeless.

To end the violence and bring peace to this mess.

A Parade of Horrible

Picture Credit: Danielle Gillard

I could not keep watching, as the scene before my eyes was so dehumanizing. I had come out determined to find AJ, but it would be impossible now amidst this chaos. The scene of it was creating major anxiety as I watched people fight and cry, trying to protect the only belongings they had to their names, and the police did not seem to care either. I wondered how they slept at night, knowing how many lives they disrupted and put at risk that day. There needs to be a better solution to this because it seems to be a never-ending war.

It's funny, this juxtaposition that I see before me. They want us to get clean and get a "real job," but when we do try, they reject us and remind us of what "we are." They do not give us a chance to reintegrate ourselves into society without making us feel ashamed of our past. Yet we all know that to move on, you must leave the past behind, so why carry it over our heads as a constant reminder? Do you not understand that those judging eyes and words are the reason we return to the Downtown Eastside? Do you know the pain of trying to be better only to get rejected and end up back where you started? We return to this community because it is the only place we are accepted, and this is amongst each other as we are always fighting against the corrupt system. Society has shunned us from any possibility of doing better, as their demeaning ways constantly remind us of separation and degradation. They sweep the streets, thinking it'll make a difference, but all it does is create turbulence and more danger for our community. The trauma of the violence and dehumanization inflicted on us is real. We never feel safe. We are all trying to survive this war in the streets, and both sides are tired, yet they will not leave us be. We are treated like animals, yet we are expected not to act like them. We are treated like a threat to society, yet we are expected not to act like it. And we are disrespected every day, yet we are expected to respect you? Democracy at its finest.

I proceeded to carefully walk down Hastings, looking for any sign of AJ. Maybe he had been hiding out in one of these tents on the street. No luck. My anxiety was bubbling as the chaos got out of control, so I decided to retreat to the Getti.

As I stepped in, I noticed the lobby was quite busy with residents, which was quite unusual. Everyone was gathered around the elevator, and they seemed to be frustrated about some event occurring there. I asked Dougy to fill me in, and he explained that a guest had a seizure in the elevator, and the staff member was told not to move the individual from the elevator. Apparently, some residents were ruthless enough to step in anyway and take a ride up to their floor with the situation happening right next to them. Eventually, someone stepped in and held the elevator doors open until the paramedics showed up, which took about 45 minutes.

"*At least the elevator is working,*" Dougy joked around, trying to lighten up the mood a little.

"*Right, it breaks down more often than it works,*" I replied with a sigh.

"*Imagine me; I'm on the fifth floor, and I've got these old, frail legs. When the elevator is broken, I cannot leave my floor. I must wait for it to be repaired, and it can take up to almost a week sometimes!*" He yelled, making sure the staff could hear him loud and clear. I felt bad for the old guy. He does not get the right support here. Being stuck in his room for a week due to the elevator breaking down is not acceptable.

"*That's so messed up, Dougy. How about I bring you up some food and weed if ever that occurs again*?" I offered with a semi-smile.

"*That would be great! What's wrong, little bird? You seem sad*," he noticed as he took hold of my hand.

"*Have you ever heard of the story about the girl who loved too much? She loved, and she loved, until she was robbed of her very last drop. With no love left for herself, she could not manage to get up. Defeated, she lay on the floor, refilling her cup, still loving the one who made her give it all up. Her love was so pure that it blinded her to the truth, making her a victim for anyone to feed from. But then, one day, the girl who loved too much grew tired and empty, and her heart started to become weary. Feeling hopeless and alone, she made herself a promise: I shall never refill my cup again, as I am better off dying with no one by my side than to die with the ones for whom I've cried.*"

"*Is that girl you, little bird?*" He followed with love and sadness in his little, old, tired blue eyes.

"*I've emptied my cup, Dougy. I've raised the white flag. For life and love has shattered my heart one too many times*," I replied to him while taking in the softness of his eyes.

"*You hold a special place in my heart, so remember that when you feel alone*," he continued while kissing the top of my hand.

"*Thanks, Dougy. I love you too*," I replied while taking his frail hands bent up from arthritis. He sang me one of his songs, and it put a smile on my face. I was grateful for this fragile old man. He always brought warmth to the coldness of my heart.

We parted ways, and I returned to my empty room.

I've been getting flashbacks from that night, and the only thing that makes them stop is when I get high. Bored and wanting to escape my thoughts, I picked up the pipe to take a hoot.

As I was about to, my phone vibrated, alerting me to a text message received by Jessy. She explained that she needed some assistance today with the animals, but truthfully, I had no more energy in me to give to anyone. I have been running on empty for a while now, and I barely have enough fuel for myself. I ignored the text and proceeded to take my hoot. That was the only thing I cared about right now. I wanted to erase all the images my eyes had captured today—in my dreams and on the streets. The heavy energies were weighing on me, and I could not bear to carry any more of this weight. This nightmare was haunting me, and everything in me wished I had never gotten those flashbacks. Though I longed for answers for so long, I now understood why AJ had a hard time telling me the truth. Sometimes, it's better to not know the truth to protect your heart. I see now that he was only protecting me while rummaging through the pain of the truth by himself. All of the guilt he was carrying drove him to insanity, and now I am slowly joining him as I sit here and wait for his return.

The next day, I woke up and craved some coffee, so I made my way down to the kitchen area. I entered and noticed a couple sitting on the couch, they were both crying and holding each other. I had a rolled joint in my pocket, so I approached them and handed it to them in hopes of cheering them up a little. They both looked up at me with broken and tired eyes. They accepted my offer and thanked me. I was not sure if they would be willing to share their agony with me, but I figured it was worth asking. Maybe they could use some extra support. At the end of the day, we all do.

"*Is everything okay? Is there anything I can do to help?*" I inquired, looking at both with concern.

"*Not anymore*," the lady answered with a quivering voice.

"*What do you mean?*" I carried on, wondering what she meant by that.

"*Have you seen the news or posters about the missing thirteen-year-old girl?*" The man asked.

"*Yes, I have, actually*," I confirmed, afraid of what I was going to hear next.

"*That's our daughter. She's been missing for nearly 5 months now, and they just found her remains in some building alongside two other bodies*," he continued as the women wept louder as he told their story. I froze, not knowing what to say, as this was truly heartbreaking to hear.

"*We tried to tell the police so many times, but they never took us seriously. If they did, she might still be here with us*," he confirmed with defeated eyes.

"*I'm... I'm so sorry. I don't know what to say*," I whispered to them. No parent should ever have to bury their kids, especially not this way.

"*There is nothing to say. All I want is justice for my daughte*r," he cried while hugging his wife.

I figured I should let them grieve in peace, so I poured myself a cup of coffee and left the kitchen area. I made my way toward Zoe's office to see if she was in today. I was running low on money, and she was still holding some of the savings, AJ and I had put aside a while ago. To my luck, she was there. I requested to retrieve the money we had saved so that I could go buy some food, weed, and whatever else I needed. She agreed, knowing legally she could not keep it from me, but I saw the disappointment in her eyes.

I left the building and made my way to the Weed Van. They sold one gram for $5, and pre-rolled joints for $4 that were dipped in THC crystals. Those were my favourites. The people working were always kind and kept the peace with the other street frolickers. After purchasing my herbs and spices, I then made my way toward the Sunrise Market on Powell Street. This was my favourite spot to go for groceries, as things were cheaply priced, though you had to eat them as soon as possible, or they would go bad. Most of their food was close to expiration, hence the price drop. But you can find some good deals and make a delicious, cheap meal. I shopped around and got some snacks for my munchies that would surely arise later.

I hurried back home, spent the night getting high on mary-jane, and ate almost everything I had bought that day.

I did not crave the harder drugs for some reason that night. My body clearly needed a break, so instead, I spent the night smoking reefer. It was nice to feel somewhat normal, though I knew it would not last. My body was still aching, and my skin felt extremely sensitive to the touch, but I tried to ignore it as much as I could. My thoughts kept jumping back to the grieving couple I had met earlier. *It's so messed up*, I whispered to myself while puffing my joint. *Illegitimi non carborundum,* I whispered as I fell asleep with food crumbs all over me.

CHAPTER 16
BINDING THE DEMONS

I woke up the next day feeling sad and longed for some company with a good joint. I attempted to call Fabian, but it went straight to voicemail. *That's a first*, I thought to myself. He always answers his phone and I have not seen him around for two or three days now. So, I made my way out of bed slowly, put on some sweatpants with a sweater, and dragged my ass all the way to the fifth floor. I had to use the stairs as the elevator was down for the fifth time this month. I hoped Fabian would be home for a nice chat about something else he was knowledgeable about. He always had a way of making me temporarily forget about the chaos among us, and I could use a little dose of that right about now. As I approached his door, I noticed it was not fully shut, which was odd for him. He was always so paranoid about people entering without permission and stealing his stuff. Ever since his weed was supposedly stolen from his freezer, he has not trusted anyone in the building.

I knocked as I called out his name but got no answer. I figured he must not have heard me since he is slightly deaf in one ear. I knocked again, and I got the same result. I began to feel a little worried; Fabian always had his phone on and his door locked. My gut was telling me I should go in just in case something had happened to him, but I also feared he would feel betrayed if I entered without his consent. I entered anyway, feeling like I should, for once in my life, listen to my gut. I opened the door and was astounded by the state of his room. I had no idea that Fabian was a hoarder, though he did always have a million new gadgets to show me, so that would make sense. I think he has been lonely ever since his wife passed away a couple of years ago. Sometimes people fill their gaps with other things than drugs, I guess.

I anxiously made my way in, trying not to step on anything of great value. The smell in his room was unbearable. It smelled like old cigarette smoke and rotten food, or worse. I covered my nose with my sweater and continued to call out his name in case he was sleeping or doing something I would rather not see. I gracefully got through the small hallway and made it to the opening of the room, and that's when I saw him. He was in a seated position on his bed, still, stiff, swollen, and purple. My mind was trying to fool my eyes with what they had just captured, but they knew better. I stood there frozen for about a minute, trying to process it all. That was the longest minute of my life. I refused to believe what I was seeing. This was my first time ever seeing a dead body, and I went into complete shock. I finally broke out of my stupor and ran down to the front desk with tears streaming down my face. Zach saw me arrive and immediately stood up, ready to come to my support. I sobbed in his arms, unable to speak and still trembling. He held me until I reached a calmer state and shared the news with him. Zach yelled for Zoe and sprinted towards the stairs. Zoe ran out in a panic, unaware of what she was about to hear. After I told her, she broke down in tears and insisted that we go up with Zach to assess the situation.

As we arrived, I could hear Zach on the phone with the 911 operator. Zoe stepped in, and I waited out in the hallway. I could not bear to see the horrific scene again. They both came back out heavy-hearted and as confused as I was. Fabian had not used it in over 15 years and did not seem to be out of character during his last days alive, so what could have happened to cause this?

We reunited in the office, waiting for the coroner and police to show up. After an hour, Zoe called a second time to follow up on their whereabouts. To our dismay, the operator announced that the call was accidentally dropped. Emotionally affected by the situation, Zoe got upset with the operator and requested that they send someone ASAP.

Another hour went by; still, no one had shown up. Zoe called again, and this time, the operator rudely told her the truth: that they had more important events to attend since the victim was already deceased. I sat in the office; my hands were uncontrollably shaking, and my mind was racing with so many questions. I feared ever more that AJ was no longer with us and up there with Fabian. I shut my eyes and attempted to erase the heartbreaking image that had intruded on my brain.

It took almost five hours for anyone to show up, and by then, I had retreated to my room, looking to numb the pain once again. I later found out that Fabian had been dead for three days, alone in his room. The footage was leaked the day after. This girl was caught on camera entering his room multiple times with his key and leaving with bags of his belongings. The staff knew how paranoid he was about anyone entering his room, so they signed an agreement not to do room checks on Fabian.

Rumour has it that she did a hot shot on him and then stole his belongings while his dead body was sitting there. It made me feel so sick to think of how desperate one can be to do such a thing. I was informed by her neighbour that her boyfriend mysteriously died the same way when he had fallen on a good amount of money, oddly enough. Fabian's street daughter later informed me that she got some people to give her a beating, which resulted in her being hospitalized. As much as I hated violence, I did not feel any empathy for her. I do believe in karma; you get what you give. Even with the footage and evidence, all the police did was knock on her door and force her to return Fabian's things. So, she had to pay for her sins someway and down here, this is the way.

I heard a knock on my door.

"*Who is it?*" I yelled out, too lazy to get up.

"*Hey Skye, it's Zoe. I just wanted to check in on you and see how you are holding up*," she said from the other side.

I forced myself up and opened the door to let Zoe in. Thankfully, I had done a major cleanup yesterday, trying to keep my mind off Fabian's death so I did not embarrass myself having her over.

"*How are you doing?*" She asked in a soft tone.

"*I've been better, I guess. It doesn't feel real. It feels like I am still processing it all*," I shared, still in disbelief of it all.

"*Yeah, that's fair. I still can't believe it, either. I always thought Fabian was going to outlast everyone here.*

I'm still trying to understand what happened to him," Zoe whispered, staring out the window.

"*Word around the block is that the girl who stole his stuff did a hot shot on him*," I replied.

"*What's a hot shot?*" She asked, curious to know more.

"*I've been told that a hot shot is when someone shoots up another person with either a bigger dose of drugs or a dose that contains fentanyl with the goal of killing the person*," I explained, disgusted by it all.

"*What? Is that some kind of sick joke?*" Zoe bleated in rage.

"*Nope, I wish it was. This is the world we live in*," I fretted, feeling helpless.

We both sat in silence for a while. It was nice to have her company. She had stopped talking to me about AJ now, understanding that I was trying to eliminate him from my thoughts. Though I knew I never could, if they believed so, they would eventually stop speaking the name that broke my heart a little more every time I heard it.

"*I heard that the cops did not do shit about it besides get her to return his belongings. I'm not sure how much of that is true, though. It doesn't do any justice to Fabian. He's still dead while she's roaming the streets for her next victim,"* I shared, breaking the silence.

"I know, the cops seem so desensitized. It's scary. I saw a video the other day about a story of this woman from the DTES who was walking down Granville Street, high out of her mind, when she accidentally stepped on a cop's shoe. His reaction was to body slam her, face down, on the ground. I understand that they probably deal with a lot of chaos from the DTES, but this is your duty to keep people safe, not to harm them or discriminate against them. And the street sweeps that just happier was so fucking dehumanizing in every way possible. They have no idea what effects this is having on their safety and mental health. I'm so over this, Skye. Everyone is at war with either themselves or people different from them. It's happening in the entire world; we are slowly destroying the planet and humankind. Now with the technology available to us, it's only going to get worse from here. Everyone is suffering. Humans are viruses. Witnessing this makes me feel like I'm about to have a burnout, to be honest with you." She wept.

"*Maybe AI wouldn't be wrong to wipe us all out*," I joked, trying to lighten the mood.

I had never seen Zoe this vulnerable before. She always carried that beautiful smile on her face. But now I could see beneath the surface that she was drowning as much as we were, in her own ways. Her heart was so big that she wanted to help as many people as she could, but she was wearing herself out. Imagine working with people where most of them are far beyond being helped and watching young ones who still have hope destroy their lives right in front of your eyes. Every day you watch people overdose; some make it, and some don't. Harm Reduction's way is not to push recovery on the users. That works for certain people, but for people like me, it only enables them. I wish we had easier access to rehab. I feel so defeated by the system, knowing the lack of support we have to get better. Yet here she was, still trying her best to save the ones she could. I sat there watching her sob and realized she had given every ounce of herself to this community yet was left with nothing. She is just another number in the system, sacrificing her sanity to save lives day after day.

I held both of Zoe's hands and looked at her directly in the eyes to make sure she would hear every word coming from my mouth.

"*Zoe, if it wasn't for you, I would have been way worse than what I am today. You have been my rock through it all, and I want you to know that I see all that you do, and I appreciate you. Let's make each other a promise. Don't let yourself be another victim of the system, and I will do the same. Fuck the system!*" I moralized, lying to myself while truly hoping for her to get out.

She smiled and gave me a long hug. We held each other and cried together, then laughed at ourselves for crying, then began to cry again. We were both so different yet also similar. I saw her, and she saw me.

Zoe left, and I stayed in my room in deep thought. I did not feel like myself. I felt like I was sitting with a stranger. I did not feel alive anymore. I felt like I was merely floating through this nightmare, waiting to wake up. But I do not wake up. This nightmare was and is my reality. The thought of this made me wonder why I was still here, waiting for a better day to come. The dangerous part of addiction lies in the synergy of loss, pain, and the need to escape. When you are lost in the meandering journey of addiction, it can be hard to find your way back.

The voices in my head and the vortex of my thoughts are now intertwined, sending me mixed messages. The fog in my mind is getting thicker. I can no longer see clearly. I am feeling these intrusive thoughts control me, and nobody can save me. My sanity is slipping away each day as I lay here in dismay at it all. Since AJ left me, sleeping, writing, and using drugs have been my only reliable analgesics.

Behind Skye's Eyes

How much of your light are you willing to dim to please the ones you love?
You give, and you give, but when it is your turn to ask for a hand to hold,
Who is there to extend theirs and walk you through it?
Do you find yourself feeling so alone that every night you have dreams reminding you of your loneliness?
My eyes have seen too much pain and sorrow for this one life.
Things nobody can or should comprehend.
I am left to carry all this weight given to me by the broken ones.
No longer resilient like I once was, I only get buried deeper.
I am exasperated in every way—emotionally, physically, and mentally.
Feeling like my fragile heart can no longer take much more before it gives up.
Every heartbeat is miraculous, as I do not know how many I have left in me.
Because even my heart is tired of breaking into pieces,
Left for me to puzzle back up on my own, only to be shattered all over again.
Eventually, the broken pieces will no longer keep the puzzle together.

The silence in the room began to play tricks on me. I swear I just heard AJ's voice. I quickly sat up and waited to see if I would hear it again, but I did not. Still convinced that I did, I waited around in the room all day, hoping he would walk through the door alive and as well as he could be.

It was Monday night, around 7 p.m., and I had left my room once to give my presence at the front desk. I scored some side, so I smoked a little hit to calm the nerves. I've switched to smoking since my arms and toes were brimming with scabs. I was not good at shooting up, so I would have to attempt it three to four times before getting it right, which left me with many scars and bruises.

For the last week, I've been hearing AJ's voice in the hallway, but every time I go out to look for him, he is already gone. I've asked the staff if he's moved into another room, and they say he hasn't, but I know they are lying. Even if that were the case, legally, they could not disclose any information without his permission. I know he is hiding from me; I hear his voice in the hallway almost every night.

I began to write on my wall until I heard a faint voice call out my name from my door. Unsure if I had heard correctly, I stayed still, waiting to hear it once more. This time I knew I had heard right.

"*Hello?*" I said out loud.

"*Skye, baby, it's me. I want to talk to you, but only like this, through the door*," I heard him say softly on the other side.

I ran to the door and laid my head on it so I could hear him better.

"*My love, I want to see you*," I pleaded.

"*I'm sorry, but I cannot face you yet. Not until I fix everything*," he responded.

"*Where have you been? I've been worried sick; I've barely been sleepin*g." I shuddered, replaying some of the harder moments I had experienced during his time away.

"*I got myself into some trouble, and I don't want to involve you. But I had to come to tell you that I still love you and that I did not leave you, Skye Baby*," he assured.

The warmth of my tears felt different this time, they were comforting. *He did not leave me*, I thought to myself.

"*I miss you so much*," I said, trying to hide the crack in my voice. I did not want him to feel bad for my pains anymore. I did not want to push him away again. I wanted him here with me. I longed for his smell, his touch, and his breath. I needed him with me more than ever.

"*When can I see you?*" I quavered, fearing the answer.

"I don't know. I don't want to make you an empty promise again, Skye Baby. But please remember that I love you, always," he replied with sadness in his voice.

It took everything in me not to swing open the door and throw myself in his arms, but I knew I had to respect his wishes. I now understood the real meaning of if you love someone, let them go. I took some deep breaths to calm my heartbeat, which felt like it was about to jump right out of my chest. After a minute or so, I realized I had heard nothing more from him.

"*AJ?*" I cautioned, afraid of the silence. Nothing.

"*AJ!*" I yelled, standing up and violently swinging the door open. He was gone.

I shut the door and broke down in tears. They were both tears of joy and pain, flowing together like a beautiful yet sad symphony. Every day after, I woke up with a little more hope that I would see him again, and now hearing his voice in the hallway brought a smile to my face. Knowing that his presence was near me brought peace and a little light to my heart, even though I could not see or feel him just yet.

I felt betrayed by Zoe. Why would she not tell me about AJ being here, knowing how worried and depressed I had been? She had seen me go through all the emotions, yet she figured not telling me was the better decision. I felt let down and concluded that I could no longer trust her, therefore I kept my distance from her after that. She questioned it at the beginning, but she eventually got the message and respected my space, sending me smiles and waves at times when she crossed my path. I ignored them, looking away and continuing on with my day. I knew it hurt her, but she hurt me, which I could not accept. She was my confidant, my rock, and she had now betrayed my trust.

I was sitting on my bed this morning, feeling my body ache from falling asleep in a horrible position. I heard a knock on my door, but I ignored it. I heard a second knock on my door, so I proceeded to yell, "*Go Away!*". That's when I heard Zoe's voice on the other side.

"*Hey, Skye, can I bother you for a sec?*" she asked. I could hear the hesitance in her voice.

I got up and opened the door.

"*Yes?*" I began while looking at her with a blank expression.

"*How have you been?*" She followed. She looked tired.

"*Fine,*" I responded coldly. I was still resentful about her betraying me.

"*Skye, did I do something to upset you?*" She inquired, longing for answers to my sudden change toward her.

"*I think you know*," I replied instantly in a passive-aggressive tone.

"*Well, that's the thing. I've been searching for any wrongdoing or something bad that I have said to you lately, but I cannot come up with anything as we have always had a good rapport*," she explained. I paused for about 15 seconds, undecided if I wanted to confront her or not.

"*Maybe it's because you lied to me about AJ, knowing you are the only person I trust here*," I finally blurted out.

"*What? AJ? I have not seen him since he went missing. Why would I lie to you about that?*" She responded, looking confused.

"*I know he is living here, in another room. I hear his voice every night in the hallways, and he spoke to me through the door the other week.*" I cried out, angry that she was still lying to my face. She stood there looking at me, but this time her look was different. I had never seen this one before.

"*May I step in so we can talk more in private?*" She requested. I accepted and let her in.

She took a seat in the chair. I sat on my bed with my feet up and my knees to my chin. I did not want to look at her. I did not want her to see me cry.

"*Skye, I am only asking this because I care for you, and I am worried about you. Have you been using more drugs lately? I am noticing that you look more tired and skinny, and you've become very irritable. Not the same Skye I first met.*" She explained with worry in her voice.

"*Ya, I have; so what? Isn't that what we are meant to do here? You give us gear to get high and a "safe space" for us to get high in. So what's the issue?* " I exhaled, annoyed by it all. She stayed quiet after my comment and kept her eyes locked on her hands.

"*Skye, would you be willing to go to the hospital with me today? Just to make sure you're healthy and doing okay*," she offered. I instantly refused.

"*I understand that hospitals aren't fun.I hate them too. But I am worried about your mental state. You mentioned you spoke with AJ the other week?*" She interrogated.

"*Yes*," I answered.

"*Did you physically see him?*" She followed.

"*No, not yet. He says he cannot face me until he fixes everything*," I disclosed, offended by her doubtful tone.

"*And you haven't spoken to him since that last interaction?*" She asked another question.

"*No, but as I said already, I hear his voice in the hallway every night*, *so I know he is here.*" I testified confidently.

"*All right, Skye, I'm going to tell you something, and it might be hard for you to hear*," she whispered with fright. I stayed in silence, waiting for her next words.

"AJ has not been here at all since his disappearance. After the day you got upset with the staff, accusing them of lying about AJ, I did my due diligence and did some investigating. Zach helped me look through the cameras, and there has never been any sign of AJ in the building since his disappearance," she carefully reported.

"*That's impossible. You're lying again!*" I yelled as I stood up with anger. How could she play with my head like that? Why had Zoe also turned against me? I know I spoke to him; we had a 4-minute conversation. I know for a fact that I heard his voice! What was she trying to do here? What game was she trying to play with me?

"*Skye, please take a breath; I beg of you*," Zoe pleaded as she also stood up in fright at my outburst. She pulled out some sheets of paper and handed them over to me with caution.

"*What the fuck is this?*" I questioned her with annoyance as I ripped them out of her hand.

"*Those are the names of all our residents here since the date you guys moved in. I have highlighted in blue the rooms where different residents have passed through, and the ones highlighted in green are the empty, vacant rooms. If AJ was staying with us, by law, we must have his information, including the room he is living in, which is your room if you look here. Do you see his name anywhere else, Skye?"* She followed; her eyes filled with concern. I started to doubt myself a little, but I still needed more proof.

I scanned every paper looking for his name, and I found nothing.

"*This can't be true*," I repeated to myself, non-stop, while looking through the list a second time with trembling hands.

"*What about the vacant rooms? He's hiding in one of those, right?*" My voice trembled, still refusing to believe her. Nothing made sense anymore. How could this be true if I had been hearing his voice every night*?* I knew the rasp and tone of his voice, like a song you had listened to a million times.

"*We can go look in them if you'd like*," she offered. I looked at the list, and we began with the closest vacant room.

Each time we opened a door, I felt myself break a little more as each room was, in fact, empty. We arrived at the last one on the list with little hope left in me; she opened the door, and I stood there in silence for a moment. I was trying to process it all, but everything felt so mixed up in my mind. I felt like I no longer knew what my reality was. I had a conversation with him, and he told me he did not leave me. This can't all be made up, can it*?*

"*Holly shit, I have officially lost my mind*," I whispered in disbelief. I had now become just like my neighbour, hearing voices and creating stories that I truly believed were real.

I broke down in tears, and Zoe held me while I drowned her shirt with my sobs. The only thing keeping me going for the last few weeks was thinking that AJ was back and I would see him again soon. Now, nothing is keeping me here. I have nothing left to lose besides my sanity, and it was already half way gone by now.

I returned to my room, still trying to understand it all. *How could this be?* This question simmered in my head all day. I decided to take a nap to rest my heavy heart. I woke up to hear voices in the hallway, and it was him. I ran to my door and swung it open. No AJ.

I hated feeling this way. I felt so lost and confused. I did not know how to make it stop, and I no longer wanted these voices to take over. It had to stop, and there was only one way I knew how to do it. I had scored some new stuff earlier from Spaz and found a hidden vein I could poke. I prepped my fix and numbed my thoughts with my sweet poison, and this became my daily routine. I no longer heard his voice in the hallway at night, which successfully set my mind at ease.

At times I stopped getting high to see if his voice was still there, but then others joined, and all the voices became clutter in my mind. Zoe says there is another way for this to go away besides getting high. She claims she can help me if I accepted her help. The truth is, I know now that nobody can save me. I'm way past gone. My only remedy is getting high to block everything and everyone out, including myself.

Rebekah BT

Nobody Belongs In an Empty Room

Picture Credit: Rebekah BT

Edited by Danielle Gillard

CHAPTER 17
IF WALLS COULD TALK

The darkness descends, and there's a creeping chill in the air. A broken heart in an empty room, with no light to shine for him to bloom. He feels crushing guilt for his actions, regretting that he allowed himself to lose control. Tears stream down his face with a flow of sorrow mixed with shame. He struggles to forgive himself, as he is to blame. He swears that he will do better and begs me for forgiveness, hoping I can look past his fucked-up ways and illness. Promises me, once again, that this will be the last time. His face begins to warp out of proportion, and his tears are now blood drops streaming down his face. He is begging me to save him, but my whole body is frozen. I cannot move, no matter how hard I try. The force of resistance wins.

The room seems to spin as his breathing is laboured and rare. I watch him lay there, lifeless but somewhat still alive in his puddle of bloody tears. The numbing sensation racing through his veins, his salvation, his crutch—all he knows for the pain. His life slowly slips away as the poison in his body seeps deeper, death ever nearer, and his future is unclear. Struggling for each breath as the darkness grows thick, the sweet surrender, at last, felt his sweet trick. I am helpless, bound to this chair, screaming in despair. His eyes begin to shut, every breath gaining more distance. My sweet love, my immersion, my dark poison.

I woke up drenched in sweat once again. This intrusive nightmare has been occurring every night for the last week. I keep dreaming that I am watching AJ slowly overdose in front of me, and I cannot do anything to help. I just simply froze while I watched him die.

Maybe this is happening because I still dream of a day when I can lay by his side, safe and free from tears, away from drugs forever more. I crave the chance to be free from this poison and to silently drift away with him for all of eternity. Despite my sorrows, I long to be enveloped by his soft touch, to live and die with the one who holds my dreams. Until then, my soul remains in darkness, yearning for each moment as it passes, hoping for a chance to escape this nightmare. I keep forgiving him, no matter how much he hurts me. Over and over. I shield him from the wrath of my inner storm, protecting him from all the pain he creates. I take my heartaches and fears with me. I bury them deep, convinced his love will keep away the tears.

I still yearn for his love, believing it will save me, yet still aware of how much it will enslave me. My life spirals into turmoil, brought upon me by his lies, but still, I stay and wait in hopes of seeing his beloved broken eyes. The ever-growing storm of wicked codependency, his embrace is no longer able to protect me from my darkness and the deceits of my mind. The thoughts and questions that cling to my every move draw me back to him even when he is not here. The chains of desire and need grip ever tighter. Both our hearts had turned to stone as our hopes and ambitions fluttered away. The beauty of our relationship faded into the depths of pain and emptiness. A vicious cycle of lies and dishonesty, leaving me alone to fight for love, forever bound to the cycle of this toxic co-dependency.

I feel lost in a dark world, consumed by my inner demons and suffering from the pain of my addiction. Amidst the chaos and despair, I still search for a light that can pull me from the depths of this agony. My reflection I cannot recognize. I can no longer stand to look in the mirror, as all I can see is a failure, a complete stranger. I have spent so many nights awake, staring out the window, listening to the lawlessness of the night's howl. Distressing screams, disagreements that result in stabbings or gunshots, police sirens singing through the city every five minutes, along with paramedics and firefighters.

How did I get here? I now walk the streets with empty eyes and a numb heart. Though I am surrounded by so many people, I still feel alone. When you give yourself so much to someone, you are left with the last crumble. They will suck you dry of your energy, leaving you to pay the fee until you have nothing left to give and are no longer able to forgive. I wish I had only kept some of that light for my days to shine bright. But it's too late now. I've reached the bottom of the pit, which is too deep to climb out. I am forgotten and broken, unable to cry for help as deaf ears and blind eyes passed me by. Every minute is a gamble for the last try and the last goodbye. I know my heart cannot take much more as it remains forever sore, and freedom is getting further away from the other side of the door.

I'm losing faith in everyone I believed in. I believed in us so much, but I see the truth now.

As the fog clears, I can see you now. But you do not see or hear me, no matter how loud I scream for you. You could not bear to drown in your misery alone. You had to pull me in with you. Your love for me is like a loathsome parasite crawling underneath my skin. Even if I cannot see you, I can always feel you around. Though deep down I do not want you there, you have imprinted yourself on me. I have tried to rid myself of you, but every time you dig your invisible fangs deeper into me. I have forgotten life before you, yet I want to erase all of you, and if deleting life completely is what it takes, then you shall have my soul to take.

I sat there on our bed with a blank stare and an empty heart, staring at these words on my walls. I had a palpable love for these words because they spoke my truth, which I could not dare speak to others. I spotted an old bubble pipe in the corner. I picked it up and smoked whatever was left in there. I then picked up the marker.

He's gone, and if I said goodbye today, tomorrow would never come. He's gone, and if I said goodbye today, my soul would be undone. I know I love you far too much, and I am clueless about knowing how to love. Too scared to face myself, I hide behind these illusions my mind has summoned. I've emptied all I had in all of you, and I am left with nothing but this hole. A trust that I dare give to you only to prove my deepest fears to be true. If only I knew how to walk away, but instead, I stay and pray that one day we will finally be okay. To my dismay, you left me. You left me here with nothing but a dirty mattress on the floor and an empty room. For the last few months, my only true friends have been these four walls. They have witnessed the depths of me more than anyone has ever stayed long enough to see. I have shared my inner thoughts on these dirty, marked walls. I have told them my darkest secrets and my deepest fears on my loneliest nights. I think that if these walls could talk, they would tell me I'm all out of luck. They would tell me that I am repelling, that nobody will ever come for me, and that I am not worthy. But if these walls could talk, maybe I wouldn't feel so alone, even if it was to remind me of the things I've done and the people I've lost.

I closed my eyes for a moment. I felt like I could hear my walls talking back to me. Maybe it's the hit I just did, but I swear I could hear them speaking. For the first time in days, I felt calm, with these walls comforting me. In your most desperate times, you will find a way to find comfort in anything. I found it in sharing my truest words on these walls. As I am breathing deeply, I hear these words playing in my head. I listened to the words my walls would say, if they could talk;

If walls could talk, I would tell her that I did not forget about her and that I was still here. I would tell her that she is beautiful. I would tell her that she is safe and that she is okay.

I've been watching her slowly self-destruct for a while now. I am afraid she will never come back. She has buried me so deep in the dark while I am still holding on to the last string of light. All I can do is hope that one day she will return to find me waiting. I hate the stench in her room. It reeks of stale urine and cigarettes. Brown tile floors, filthy from collecting the dirt and bugs she carries in with her shoes. Broken pipes and used needles rest in each corner, slowly accumulating as the days go by. The once white walls are now yellow from the smoke and smothered in writings; she writes on them when she is strung out, her words always so sad and bitter. Nobody belongs in an empty room. Her only companions are the cockroaches roaming around, feeding off her dirt and rotten food.

She's gone, and it will never be the same. She's gone, and if I call her name, she won't come for me. She will never bat an eyelash in my direction. A fragile soul, a fouling meek mind with bitter, heartless words. So much denial, so much contradiction, and so much instability. She's gone, but I know she can make it back. I want to tell her she does not have to inject her veins with this poison to ease her pain. She has tainted all that she loves with her darkness, and she is no longer resisting the fight. I resist her darkness, but I also welcome her with her writings on the wall.

She fights off the pain and tears as she tries not to break, but it feels like all her strength is being sucked away.

Shallow thoughts piercing through a shallow heart, a masterpiece, a somber work of art. The senseless days are starting to feel a little too comfortable. The fog in her mind seeps through the gaps and fills them with numbness. Pain always leaves its mark and never really fades. Just another poison to add to her bitter heart. Danger lurks in the shadows while life escapes you right before your eyes.

The dirty mattress on the floor is covered with burn holes. I watch her lay there, looking up at the ceiling. I wish I knew what she was thinking. I wish she could hear me. Oh, if walls could talk. She sits up, opens her small metal box, and pulls out a little baggie. She flicks the bag to see what is left of her stash. She has been isolated here for months now. She empties her drugs into the cooker, lights a candle, and holds it over the flame. Her eyes fixed on the rock, which was slowly melting and beginning to bubble. Her heart is beating stronger as she inhales the scent of her wicked enemy. Her hands are trembling from sleep deprivation and lack of food, and she almost spills the liquid. She puts the cooker down, takes the cap off the needle, pierces through the cotton, and gradually fills it with the venom. She wraps a tie around her right arm, as her left arm has retired due to the abuse of the needle. Only to be left with the scars exposing her silent agony.

She closes her eyes and takes a deep breath. I can see a tear making its way down her cheek. She is mumbling words I wish to hear, but I cannot. I can only watch her battle her inner demons, hoping today, she will finally win.

If walls could talk, I would tell her this is not the way, this does not have to be the screenplay, and this does not have to be her last day. I would tell her that her time is fading away, along with her soul. I would tell her that I still think she is beautiful. But I can no longer tell her that she is safe and okay.

I've been watching her slowly self-destruct for a while now, and I know she will never come back. She has shunned me from any possibility of making it out of this darkness. Her eyes are so empty you can't bear to stare. Her tears only appear when she is sober, which makes her sick. Dope sick. Her smile no longer has a presence, hiding the rancid teeth that inhibited her mouth. Her skin was as white as the snow, brimming with scars and scabs. Her arms, hands, feet, and toes were filled with them, and she no longer tried to hide them.

Her body was a victim of her sins, her heart was a victim of her pains, and her soul was a victim of her darkness.

Venom injected; she was too weak to resist, losing herself in the abyss. And here I am, left to wonder: will she have the chance to write words on me again? Or will this be the end of her story on these walls? Her last chance, her last dance.

Knock, knock, knock.

"Hey Skye, room check!", Zoe shouts across the door, but I cannot answer her.

Knock, knock, knock.

"Skye, I'm coming in," she followed.

Zoe opens my door and walks in.

Doug – Your Neighbourhood just got dope

Downtown EastSide Art *Downtown Eastside Creativity*

Picture Credit: Danielle Gillard

Bangtown Building

Broken Piano

Picture Credit: Rebekah BT

Edited By: Danielle Gillard

Hastings

Picture Credit: Dave Taillefer

Edited By: Danielle Gillard

Printed in the USA
CPSIA information can be obtained
at www.ICGtesting.com
LVHW052322291223
767736LV00013B/591

9 781962 381147